ALSO BY PATRICIA WILLIS

Out of the Storm
A Place to Claim as Home

DANGER *ALONG THE*
OHIO

BY PATRICIA WILLIS

CLARION BOOKS
New York

Clarion Books
a Houghton Mifflin Company imprint
215 Park Avenue South, New York, NY 10003
Text copyright © 1997 by Patricia Willis
Text type is 13.5/16.5-point Dante

For information about this and other Houghton Mifflin
trade and reference books and multimedia products, visit
The Bookstore at Houghton Mifflin on the World Wide Web
at ⟨http://www.hmco.com/trade/⟩.

Printed in the USA

Library of Congress Cataloging-in-Publication Data

Willis, Patricia.
    Danger along the Ohio / by Patricia Willis.
        p.   cm.
    Summary: Lost in the Ohio River Valley in May 1793, twelve-year-old
Clare and her two brothers struggle to survive in the wilderness and to avoid
capture by the Shawnee Indians.
    ISBN 0-395-77044-0
    [1. Survival—Fiction.   2. Brothers and sisters—Fiction.   3. Ohio River Valley—
History—To 1795—Fiction.   4. Shawnee Indians—History—To 1795—Fiction.
5. Indians of North America—Ohio River Valley—History—To 1795—Fiction.] I. Title.
PZ7.W68318Dan   1997
[Fic]—dc20   96-42174
                                                                        CIP
                                                                        AC

BP   10   9   8   7   6   5   4   3   2   1

For Nikki, Colleen, and Tim—
embrace the opportunities.

CHAPTER 1

≈≈≈≈≈≈≈≈≈≈≈≈≈≈≈≈≈≈≈

"You young 'uns get inside—hurry!"

At his father's command, Amos scooped up his marbles and ducked into the boat cabin. Jonathan and Clara came scrambling in behind him. Over and over again, they'd been warned that such an order must be obeyed without question and without delay.

Fingers trembling, Amos fed the marbles into the pouch secured on his belt and tightened the drawstring. Then he crept back to the patch of sun slanting in the doorway. Had his father seen some real Indians? Forced into a narrow channel between an island and the riverbank, the flatboat skimmed dangerously close to shore. To Amos, it looked like an ideal place for an ambush.

"See anything?" Jonathan asked, edging near the door.

"Nothing yet," Amos replied, glancing over at his brother. Though only seven years old, Jonathan looked like a little old man in the beaver hat he wore from dawn to dark. Something in his face always reminded Amos of their mother. She'd died giving birth to Jonathan, and at first Amos and Clara had resented the helpless baby who had taken her away from them. But their resentment didn't last. Jonathan needed them so desperately, and his need seemed to soothe their own raw hurting. Together they'd learned to live without their mother.

"Why are the Indians after us, Amos?"

Jonathan's hushed question brought Amos back to the unseen danger on the river. Their father had said there would be Indians, but he'd also assured them that a home in the Ohio wilderness was worth a slight risk. After helping a neighbor family move to their land in the Ohio country, he'd returned with glowing descriptions of fertile soils and trees over a hundred feet tall. It wasn't long before he began to talk of moving the family west.

"Why do the Indians hate us?" Jonathan persisted.

"They don't understand us owning the land," Amos said, repeating what his father had told him. "Or living on it all our lives. They use the land but they don't own it. They're worried that if people keep coming, they'll get pushed out."

"But there's plenty of land for everyone," Jonathan said. "Just look at it." He waved an arm at the green, rolling forest stretching from horizon to horizon.

Amos sucked in a breath and grabbed Jonathan's shoulder. "Look. Do you see them?"

"Indians? Where?"

Amos leveled an arm through the doorway, pointing at the riverbank. "There . . . under the trees. There's five or six of them, maybe more." Lean dark forms slipped along in the dense shade, keeping pace with the flatboat. Sometimes they faded out of sight, but then they would reappear, silent, hounding shadows among the trees.

At Pittsburgh, Amos had heard the men talking about raids up and down the Ohio River. Suspecting that the flatboats were bringing people to settle on their land, the Indians followed the boats downstream, waiting for them to come close to shore. Then they attacked without mercy. But the boatmen were mindful of the dangers. They kept their flatboats in the middle of the river, constantly studying the riverbanks and the shaded coves along them. And they always tied up on the Virginia side—the eastern side—at night.

Amos spent much of his time scanning the forests, too. Not only was he curious about the

Indians, but at least once a day his father reminded him that seeing before you were seen could mean the difference between life and death in this wild country.

"What'll we do if they swim out to the boat?" Jonathan asked through chattering teeth.

Before Amos could answer him, Clara crowded between them in the door opening.

"The savages will be well advised to keep their distance," she said. "Papa showed me how to use his pistol. I haven't had much practice, but I can hit an Indian if I have to."

Amos stared at his sister and shook his head. She was twelve, only a year younger than Amos, and bold as brass. But despite her sassiness and her endless talking, he was usually glad to have her around. Especially after that awful time last September. When he'd remained silent for days, Clara had understood and left him alone. When he'd lost his direction and his will, she'd told him what to do. When others had pried and prodded, she'd protected him. Through it all, she'd been his faithful friend.

From the moment his father had mentioned they might move, Amos had waited impatiently for the day they would leave. He'd hoped that new people and new places would wipe away the bad memories. But it hadn't happened. Even now, he was torn between wanting to remember and wanting to forget. Would he ever be able to think of his friend Simon without trembling like an aspen leaf?

"I wish we'd never come out here," Jonathan mumbled.

"As long as Papa's here, we don't need to worry," Clara said, frowning at him.

"But Jimmy Larkin told me that the Indians—"

"Sassafras!" Clara broke in. "Jimmy Larkin wouldn't know an Indian from an elderberry bush."

"Look, they've stopped," Amos said. He pointed to the shadowy figures at the forest's edge, as motionless as rocks. Suddenly the boat came alive with loud voices, then footsteps on the cabin roof and the creak of the steering oars.

"Wheeling Island dead ahead," shouted one boatman.

Amos let out a slow breath. The Indians didn't dare attack this close to a settlement. He glanced back at the spot where he'd last seen them. Maybe he only imagined a lone figure there under the trees, his rifle raised in a silent threat.

Their father leaned into the doorway. "They won't bother us now," he said, indicating it was safe for Amos and the others to come out on deck. Then he went forward to help the boatmen.

Edging out into the sunshine, Amos leaned

against one of the crates crowding the afterdeck. From bow to stern, the flatboat was crammed with supplies for the people downriver. He'd heard of the few isolated settlements below Marietta. They had foreign, tongue-twisting names—Cincinnati, Gallipolis. Rivers emptying into the Ohio bore Indian names equally difficult to pronounce, Muskingum, Tuscarawas, Olentangy.

The strange names as well as the shadowy forests were a constant reminder that they were entering an unknown world. Back home in eastern Pennsylvania, Amos had voiced his fears of wild animals and Indians. His father had reassured him.

"Twenty, thirty years ago it would've been dangerous to live in the Ohio country," he'd said. "But it's 1793, and there are towns there now, and forts. And more people moving in every day. Don't fret. By midsummer we'll be settled and secure. We'll have a cabin built and corn growing."

But bad weather had delayed their departure from Pennsylvania, and swollen mountain streams had hindered their travel west. It was already the middle of May and they were still on the river. Even after they got off the boat at Marietta, it would take several more days to reach our land. We're a long way from planting corn, Amos thought.

Clara came and plopped down on the crate next

to him, pulling her linsey-woolsey skirt up to her knees. Her hair, naturally curly and fine as lamb's wool, shone like gold in the sun. "Let me have your knife, Amos."

"What for?" he demanded. He didn't like anyone using his knife. He'd worked too long and hard to get it, husked corn three days in a row. He carried it with him everywhere in a leather sheath on his belt. It was thin and sleek, with a white bone handle and a blade honed razor-sharp.

"Look at my fingernails." Clara stretched her hands out in front of her. The nails were jagged and broken, some down to the quick. "I look like a muskrat that's been caught in a trap and tried to chew its paws off to get loose."

Amos grinned at her. She was more worried about her fingernails than she was about the pursuing Indians. He pulled out the knife and handed it to her. "Be careful and don't drop it overboard."

Clara talked as she whittled at her nails. "Papa says we'll be in Marietta in a couple more days. If the river stays high and there's no fog. Do you reckon there'll be Indians near our land, Amos? Do you think . . . ."

Knowing that Clara's questions seldom required answers, Amos stopped listening and gazed downstream at Wheeling Island. A stone's throw from the Virginia shore, it looked like many other willow islands they'd passed, but bigger, and there were cabins on it. He could see figures scurrying to and fro. They looked small next to the great Virginia mountain looming over them like a bear over an anthill.

The flatboat rode lightly, both pushed and carried by the boiling, brawling river. On the cabin roof, the boatmen waited for the right moment to ply their oars, then, with skillful strokes, aimed their craft at the island's narrow landing.

Shaggy, bearded men came running down to the river's edge. "Welcome to Wheeling town," they shouted over the water. As soon as the boat touched land, eager hands pulled it close and tied it up. Then the boatmen laid down two thick planks from the deck to the shore.

Clara came to stand beside Amos. "Don't you think they're being a little presuming, to call this place a town?" She handed him the knife and moved toward the cattle pen on the back of the boat. Their Jersey cow, undisturbed by the bustle and noise, stood patiently waiting for Clara to attach the lead rope.

Amos had thought his sister was raving mad to insist on bringing a cow into the wilderness, though he knew she loved that animal as much as some girls loved their homemade rag dolls. To everyone's surprise, the cow caused no trouble at all. She walked alongside Clara, without a lead rope much of the time, crossing mountains and hollows with equal ease. Even the streams were no obstacle to her. She was a better swimmer than many of the humans she followed. And despite the long, hard journey, she was still giving milk.

As soon as Clara led Queen Anne down the ramp, the cow dropped her head and began to graze in the knee-high grass on the island. The boys followed, pausing to watch the men wrestle several barrels and crates ashore. One of the boatmen pointed upstream, telling about the pursuing Indians. The townsmen didn't seem worried and their casual acceptance of the news made Amos breathe easier.

"Let's look around," he said to Jonathan, and they set off to explore the island.

"Don't take such big steps, Amos," Jonathan said. "I want to practice Indian walking." Someone had told them that Indians walked single file in the woods, each person in line stepping in the leader's tracks. Looking at the single set of footprints, a person wouldn't know how many Indians had passed there. Amos and Jonathan had tried it just to break the monotony on the journey west, but they weren't very good at it.

"We'd better not get too far from the town," Jonathan said, when they lost sight of the cabins. "There might be Indians."

"There aren't any Indians here," Amos said.

"There's always Indians on this side of the mountains," Jonathan murmured. "That's what Papa says."

Amos walked on in silence. Their father only said that to remind them to be on their guard. But here on the island, among these unfearing woodsmen, they needn't worry about Indians.

As Amos watched a flock of geese settle down on the Ohio, Jonathan scampered up into a willow tree that leaned over the water. The branch creaked beneath him and when it dipped toward the water, he scurried back to land. Amos grinned to himself. His brother was as much at ease in a tree as he was on the ground. And there was certainly no shortage of trees for him to climb in the Ohio country.

When the boys returned to the boat, one of the boatmen directed them to a nearby cabin where supper was being prepared. Inside, Amos saw Clara at the hearth, helping a big-faced, boisterous woman the men called Lizzie. Amos was surprised there were no other women there, and no children either. After all, this was supposed to be a real town.

The meal was mostly meat and fowl: venison, squirrel, turkey, partridge. What Amos liked best were the flat cakes of skillet bread, so hot that he tossed them between his hands to cool them. For dessert, Lizzie served squares of dough filled with dried apples and honey. It was the best meal Amos had eaten since they'd left their home in Pennsylvania.

When Lizzie learned that the cow she'd seen grazing belonged to Clara, she tried to persuade Clara to sell her. Clara just laughed and shook her head.

"I'll give you a clock I brought from Virginny," Lizzie pleaded. "And a crock of honey. I'll even throw in a little she-coon I tamed."

"There's nothing in the whole world I'd take for Queen Anne," Clara told her.

Soon after supper the whiskey jugs were brought out, a signal for Clara and Jonathan and Amos to return to the flatboat. Afraid that Queen Anne would wander into the river in the dark, Clara brought the cow and tethered her to a tree near the boat.

It was a warm May night with the river murmuring past and little waves slapping against the boat planks. The three of them lay on their blankets in the boat cabin, listening to the night sounds, swatting at the pesky mosquitoes.

Amos never fell asleep without thinking of his friend Simon, but maybe in their new home he'd be able to forget. Maybe his family could forget, too. They tried to conceal their thoughts, but sometimes he could see the remembrance in their eyes.

To keep from thinking of Simon, Amos recalled the tale he'd heard of two white boys captured by the Shawnee years before in western Pennsylvania. The older boy, fascinated with Indian life, had struck a bold bargain with the Shawnee. He'd promised he would go with them peacefully if they would set his brother free. Admiring the boy's courage, the Indians had agreed. Returning with him to their village, they had accepted the boy into their tribe, taught him Indian ways, and years later, in a gesture of great respect, made him a chief.

As he lay there in the darkness, Amos thought of the boy who had traded his own life for his brother's. He'd become the famous warrior chief, Blue Jacket. Did he ever, Amos wondered, think of his real family and long to see them? I'm going to live in a strange place, he mused, but I'll have my family with me. Amos always felt safe with his father. He heard a whippoorwill call and another answer from farther away before his eyes closed and he slept.

The moment he woke, Amos knew something

was wrong. He heard men shouting, then jumped at the sickening sound of gunshots. Springing to the open door, he looked out into a night filled with noise and flashing lights. Clara and Jonathan came up behind him, watching the bursts of light that signaled gunshots even before they heard the sound. Like a beaver tail smacking water, a warning shout rang through the night. "Indians!"

Amos shrank back between Clara and Jonathan. Sharp, booming explosions of gunfire stabbed him like a knife and he clapped his hands over his ears to shut out the sounds. If he couldn't hear the guns, maybe he wouldn't have to remember Simon.

A long, agonizing time passed before he realized that Clara had disappeared. He grabbed Jonathan. "Where is she?"

"She went to get Queen Anne."

Amos peered toward shore and saw her pulling the cow up the ramp. "She's clear daft," he muttered. The cow's heavy hoofs clattered on the deck and Amos sucked in his breath and held it. The sound was loud enough to be heard, even over the gunshots.

As Clara led the cow into the pen, he crept over to her. "You'd risk your life for that dumb animal!" he burst out.

"She's not dumb," Clara spat back at him. "And if you think I'll let those savages—"

Jonathan appeared beside them. "Hush, Sister. They'll hear you."

Clara pushed Jonathan aside. "I'm getting Papa's pistol," she declared, and slipped inside the boat cabin. A moment later she reappeared, holding the gun in both hands.

Amos cringed from the ugly weapon. If there was any shooting, Clara would have to do it. He couldn't . . . he could never pick up a gun again!

Suddenly, the boat rocked toward the shore. Someone had come on board.

CHAPTER 2

"Get down!" Clara said and pushed Jonathan into the hay beside Queen Anne. The cow had already lain down and they huddled against her, staring into the darkness, hardly breathing.

There was a crash of boards, then scuffling noises. Amos guessed some Indians had come on board and were breaking open the supply crates stacked in front of the cabin. It wouldn't be long until they came to see what else they could find.

Amos folded his arms across his chest to stop his shivering. If they could get to the island and find their father, they'd be safe. Tied at the bow and stern, the boat lay close to the land. All they had to do was slip over the side and wade to shore. But then they must try to reach one of the cabins without being seen. Right now, Amos's legs felt as useless as dead logs.

Clara grabbed his shoulder, echoing his own thoughts. "We've got to get over to the island." As Amos started to stand up, she grabbed his arm. "Wait!" When she began piling hay close around Queen Anne, Amos realized what she was trying to do. The Jersey cow was almost the same color as the hay, and partially concealed, she might not be noticed in the darkness. Amos bent to help Clara, gritting his teeth when he thought about the three of them with no place to hide.

As they rose and crept across the deck, the scuffling noises on the front of the boat ceased. "We'll never make it," Clara whispered and motioned them back to the stern railing. "Get into the water and hang on to the boat," she directed.

Amos didn't hesitate. Clara had decided almost everything these past months, and he seldom questioned her decisions. Ever since the accident, he'd been afraid of doing the wrong thing. Now, almost numb with fear, he was relieved to have someone else tell him what to do.

Like lizards slithering across a rock, they slipped over the railing and lowered themselves into the black water. Even this close to shore, the river ran deep and the powerful current tugged at their legs. The water was cold, too, though Amos knew that wasn't the reason for his chattering teeth. He clamped his jaws tight and eased downward until only his head was above water.

The steady clatter of gunfire continued, as terrifying to Amos as the Indians. Over the top of the railing, the three of them watched a burning cabin send explosions of sparks up into the black sky. Smoke hovered over the island like night fog.

As Clara shifted the pistol from one hand to the other, it struck the boat with a dull thud. She hissed in a breath and sank lower in the water.

At that moment, Amos saw a movement above him. He pulled Jonathan closer to the boat and flattened himself against the thick timbers. An Indian stood on the cabin roof, clad only in breechcloth and leggings and carrying a hatchet. His lean body glistened in the glaring light.

They'd seen Indians at Pittsburgh, shiftless, slouching men who loitered in doorways and begged money for whiskey. Their father had told them the whiskey lured the Indians away from their own people. It made them useless and dependent on the white men. The man looming over Amos was different. He had a power and command those begging Indians lacked, and a fierceness that scared Amos down to the ends of his toes.

Amos could almost feel the Indian's eyes probing the night. If he came down on the afterdeck, the three of them would have to swim away and try to escape in the darkness. As Clara and Jonathan pressed in under the boat, Amos gulped a silent breath and settled into the water. It closed over him with a gentle touch. He stayed submerged as long as he could, then, lungs aching for release, floated upward.

The Indian was still there, but he seemed hypnotized by the frenzied activity around the burning cabins. When a voice sounded nearby, he moved across the roof and disappeared.

"He's gone," Amos whispered, though vibrations through the boat timbers told him someone else was still on board.

Amos's throat was so dry he couldn't even swallow. His fingers ached from their vise-like grip on the boat and his arms and legs moved in an uncontrollable shivering. If the other Indian came to search the rest of the boat, he wasn't sure he'd be able to move at all.

Just then, someone on the island screamed in pain. Amos shuddered and leaned toward Clara. "I wonder if Papa . . ."

"Of course he's all right," she said. "He'll come for us as soon as the Indians go away."

What if they didn't go away? Amos wanted to ask her, but he kept silent. They were safe for the moment, shrouded by the deep night shadows. He tried not to think of what might happen at sunrise.

There were no sounds on the boat now. Even the vibrations had stopped. With deliberate, snail-like movement, Amos raised up and peered across the deck toward the island. Then he froze! The Indian he'd seen on the cabin roof was there on shore only a few feet away. The boat's mooring rope dangled from his hand. As Amos watched, the man tossed the rope into the water, then gave the boat a hard shove with his foot. The craft floated silently away from the island.

Suddenly, the Indian spied Amos. In that awful moment, Amos couldn't even muster the strength to duck out of sight.

The Indian sprang into the water, lunging for the derelict boat, but he was too late. It had slipped beyond his reach. Seconds later, the craft was captured by the mighty flow of the river and skimmed away into the night. A fluttering breath escaped Amos's lips. If the Indian had seen him a moment sooner, they'd be prisoners now, or maybe worse.

"What's happening?" Clara whispered.

"The boat . . . it's . . . we're moving," Amos said.

Still clinging to the stern railing, the three of them stared back at the receding island and the Indian outlined in firelight. Then they became aware of the swirling, dragging water. The river's powerful current threatened to tear them from the boat.

"Come on," Clara said, and still holding the loaded pistol, she clawed her way up out of the water and onto the deck. Amos and Jonathan were right behind her. Wet and shivering, they turned again toward the island's fading lights and sounds.

The clatter of gunfire was softer now, muted by distance, and the fires merged into a single glow that grew ever smaller in the darkness. They couldn't seem to take their eyes off that diminishing point of light.

Amos's chest tightened when he thought about what had happened. They had escaped the Indians, but in the process, they'd lost their father. He was still there on the island, fighting for his life. Amos bowed his head, wondering if they would ever see him again. The thought of losing him brought back hurting memories of Simon. He tried to push away that awful day but it was as real as the Indian attack.

They'd been playing pirates, pretending the apple tree and the woodpile were ships. He could see Simon standing in the crotch of the tree, legs widespread, hands on his hips, laughing down at him. "Heave to and prepare to be boarded," came his blustering command.

Amos had jumped down from the woodpile and run into the house, looking for something, anything that would help make him the conqueror. He spied his father's pistol resting on wooden pegs over the mantel. It had hung there untouched for years, a rusty relic of earlier, more dangerous times. They'd all been warned never to touch it, but Amos had forgotten in the heat of the game. Carrying it outside, he'd aimed the pistol at Simon and shouted, "Bang, you're dead!" When he squeezed the trigger, the gun fired and the bullet struck Simon in the stomach.

Nobody had blamed him, not even Simon, though sometimes Amos wished they had. Someone had to take the blame, and he knew it was his fault.

Day after day, Simon had lain there, weak and helpless against the pain. At first, Amos had visited him every day, refusing to believe that his friend was losing his fight for life. But finally, there came the moment when he had to admit the truth. The next day he couldn't gather the courage to face Simon. Instead, he sought solace in the woods, trying to hide from what he knew was happening. When he returned home that evening at dusk, his father told him that Simon was dead.

The sound of Jonathan slapping a mosquito brought Amos back to the drifting boat. Thoughts of Simon faded as he considered their predicament.

He and his brother and sister were on their own now, but at least they were alive and free. When daylight came, they could steer the boat to shore. Once safe on land again, they could decide what to do, whether to walk back to Wheeling or try to take the boat back upriver. Clara would know what was best.

"Amos . . . look!" Clara was staring toward the front of the boat, her eyes circles of light in the darkness.

Amos spun around, sucking in his breath when he saw a bright red glow lighting up the night and blazing in the water. Fire!

The three of them scrambled up on the cabin roof and stared down at the forward deck. Flames had consumed the piles of hay the boatmen used for their beds, and now they crawled toward the splintered crates. Even the deck timbers were smoldering, fanned by the wind off the river.

For several moments, the three of them stood there, too stunned to think, to reason. Clara was the first to move. She leaped down on the forward deck and grabbed a tattered blanket, then ran to the railing and doused it in the water. Dashing across the deck, she flailed the blanket at the creeping tongues of fire.

Amos remembered that a bucket always hung on

a peg at the forward corner of the cabin. He ran to the edge of the roof, but it wasn't there. The Indians must have taken it. He rushed to the cabin for more blankets, and he and Jonathan went to help Clara.

They fought a losing battle. The fire spread quickly and when flames licked up the front of the cabin, Amos knew the flatboat would soon be a floating inferno. They wouldn't be able to stay on board much longer.

"If we could get in close to the shore . . ." he said to Clara.

She gazed at him, her wet hair straggling across her face. Then, pointing toward the cabin roof, she dropped her hands to her sides. "The oars are gone," she said.

As the fire gained in fury, the three of them retreated to the afterdeck. Queen Anne was on her feet now, gazing at the menacing glow, her eyes reflecting the red, flaring light. Clara draped her arm around the animal's neck. Then, as though the three of them all had the same thought, they stared back upriver.

The light on the island was no longer visible. There was nothing to see now but a wall of darkness pushed back only a little by the raging fire on the boat.

Amos could feel the heat of it. Smoke wafted over him and made his eyes water and his nose burn. They'd have to swim soon. In his mind he saw the river as it had looked in the afternoon, a stream so wide that trees along the distant banks appeared no bigger than pasture weeds. They were all good swimmers, but could they swim that far? Could they even find the river bank in the dark?

"If we wait a little longer," he said, "we might drift close to shore."

"We can't wait long," Clara replied. "The boat's burning like a summer haystack."

"What about Queen Anne?" Jonathan asked in a high, quavering voice.

"Don't worry about her," Clara said, with a hint of anger in her voice. "She's a better swimmer than you are."

"How can we find land if we can't even see it?" Jonathan murmured.

Clara reached out and laid a hand on his shoulder. "Just stay close to Queen Anne when we get in the water. You can hold onto her tail. She won't mind."

They watched the fire creeping along the edges of the cabin roof. "My knapsack!" Clara exclaimed and bolted for the cabin door. Moments later, she emerged, coughing and rubbing her eyes, her knapsack slung over one shoulder. She stooped and picked up the pistol. "We might need this," she said to Amos.

"You can't swim with that," he said. "You'd sink like a rock. Besides, the powder'd get wet." Here in the Ohio country, Amos had noticed that every man carried some kind of weapon, for hunting and for protection. But what good was a gun that wouldn't fire? Clara ignored him, pushing the pistol deep into her knapsack.

When the hay inside the cabin finally ignited, hot air exploded through the doorway and threw burning ashes over them. Amos slapped at the feathers of smoke rising from his shirt, while Clara brushed sparks off of Queen Anne's back.

There wasn't much time left, Amos knew. He peered into the darkness, hoping for a glimpse of land. Although the river flowed almost straight south here, the boatmen, and their father too, had insisted on calling the west bank the north bank. Amos guessed it was because farther on, the river angled west toward the Mississippi. Now, facing downriver, Amos knew that somewhere to his left lay the south bank of the river. They'd be safe on the south bank.

Clara grabbed Queen Anne's rope and led her to the opening in the stern railing. With a thick lump in his throat, Amos joined her and Jonathan. Water sloshed over the deck timbers at their feet, reminding them of the river's might. If only they could see the land!

The hay in the cowpen caught fire and flames soared into the black sky. The heat now was almost unbearable.

"I think it's time." Clara's wide eyes met Amos's.

"I reckon so," Amos said.

Just as Clara started to push Queen Anne into the water, her hand jerked upward. "There's the bank! I see trees."

Amos looked where she pointed. Faint, gray shapes swam at the edge of the darkness, like storm clouds on a far horizon. "But Clara, that's the north bank," he shouted. "We can't go—"

"Sassafras! I don't care what bank it is," she said. "It's solid ground and it's close. Come on, Jonathan."

She pulled on Queen Anne's rope and the cow pranced away from the flames, then tossed her head and plunged into the river. Clara grabbed Jonathan's hand and jumped in after her. The current swept them away from the boat and in only seconds they had disappeared. Amos gulped a quick breath and hurled himself after them.

CHAPTER 3

$\approx\approx\approx\approx\approx\approx\approx\approx\approx\approx\approx\approx\approx$

Expelling the last of his air, Amos fought his
way to the surface. For an instant he glimpsed the
boat's fiery glow, then the night closed around him,
as black as the watery world below him. He felt the
current carrying him downstream and was tempted
to ride the buoyant flow, but he knew he must get
to land. He struggled across the current, swimming
hard.

Just then, something struck his shoulder and he
went under. A heavy, rolling log bumped and buf-
feted him until finally he grabbed hold of it. He
clung to the log, coughing up water, gasping for air.
When he could breathe again, he let go and struck
out for the invisible shore. He had to reach land
soon or he'd be miles downstream from Clara and
Jonathan. Then he might never find them.

When his reaching fingers brushed against wet,

slippery leaves, he let his legs sink downward until his bare feet touched something solid. There it was—the muddy bank of the river! Floundering through the shallow water, he collapsed face-down in the tall reeds.

Several minutes passed before his heart stopped pounding and he gathered the strength to sit up. As he gazed toward the sound of the whispering river, he glimpsed movement, and a pale reflection. Day was coming at last. Minute by minute more of the sweeping river became visible. The brightening sky revealed mists drifting over the water like ragged, wind-stirred curtains.

As it grew light, Amos's gaze followed the river-bank northward, searching, hopeful. Then his breath eased out in a long, shuddering sigh. A quarter mile or so upstream he glimpsed Clara among the waving reeds, her knees pulled up to her chin and her head and arms resting on them. He couldn't see Jonathan or Queen Anne, but they must be nearby.

Amos sprang to his feet and hurried toward her. When he came near and saw her face, he stopped. "What is it?" he asked.

"Oh, Amos, Jonathan's gone . . . and Queen Anne. I was right next to him," she said. "He was holding on to Queen Anne's tail, but I got too close to her hoofs and went under. When I came up, they were both gone."

"Jonathan's a good swimmer," Amos said. "He's around here somewhere. We can holler for him."

"No!" Clara said. "I've been thinking about what you said just before we jumped, about this being the north shore. We'd better stay quiet. We don't want the Indians to hear us." She picked up her knapsack and rose to her feet. "Come on," she said. "We've got to find Jonathan."

They clambered up the weedy bank to a flat shelf overlooking the river. It gave them a good view of the riverbank in both directions, but there was no sign of Jonathan or the cow.

"They have to be farther downstream," Clara said. She pointed to where the river wound westward out of sight. "The current may have carried them around the bend." Not waiting for Amos, she headed in that direction.

Amos hurried after her, remembering the urgent pull of the river and his own desperate struggle to reach land. How could a small boy resist the river's power? He can't have drowned, he told himself. After losing their father, they couldn't lose Jonathan too.

Amos stopped when he saw Clara kneel beside a small stream and drink from her cupped hands. He joined her, grateful for the cool water that soothed away the dryness in his throat.

As Clara splashed water on her face, Amos stood and looked around. He squinted, welcoming the sun's warmth, while his keen eyes scanned the riverbank for some sign of Jonathan. He couldn't see far because of the trees, but there was something up ahead, a slight movement among the bushes. For several moments he studied the spot. Then he drew a deep breath and released it. What he saw was the repeated flick of Queen Anne's ears. He pulled Clara to her feet and pointed, then they both took off running.

Drawing near, they found the Jersey lying beneath a giant sycamore, her eyes closed, head drooping. Jonathan lay curled up asleep against her flank, his head resting on his beaver hat. Their rustling steps roused Queen Anne, and her soft brown eyes settled on them only a moment before closing again.

"Let them sleep," Clara whispered. Amos nodded and they turned and walked out to the sunlit rim of the river. Clara sat down on a fallen tree while Amos stood staring out at the Ohio.

Green hills cradled the broad river, with sunlight splintering the water into tiny, sparkling shards. Amos recalled the storekeeper at Pittsburgh telling him about the river running past his doorstep. He'd said the English called it Ohio, a form of the Indian word, O-Y-O, meaning great river. He'd added that the French called it *La Belle Rivière*, the beautiful river. Whatever its name, the river wrapped Amos in its soft, soothing grandeur.

"What are we going to do, Amos?" The tone of Clara's voice shattered the sunny peace.

Amos centered his thoughts on her urgent question. Now that they were safe on shore and all together again, they faced other problems. They had survived the Indian raid and the burning raft and the river, but they were on the Ohio's perilous north bank. The Indians claimed this land, and stubbornly defended it.

They were lost and alone, and they had nothing except what was in Clara's knapsack. There had been plenty of things on the boat they could have used: an ax, shoes, food. No use crying over spilt milk, Amos thought, then felt a surge of hope as he remembered Queen Anne. Her milk would keep them from starving until they found their father.

"You think we should head back to Wheeling?" he asked.

"You mean go back where the Indians are?" Clara countered.

"Shouldn't we try to find Papa?"

"How would we get over to the island?" Clara demanded.

"But what else can we do?" Amos flung his arms wide, impatient with all the questions and no answers.

"We can go on to Marietta," Clara said at last. "Papa is sure to come looking for us downriver when he sees the boat is gone."

"How can we find Marietta?" Amos questioned. "There's nothing but woods for hundreds of miles."

"Papa said it was on the north bank. All we need to do is follow the river until we come to it."

"But Clara, there's Indians here, and all kinds of wild animals . . . bears . . ."

"Sassafras! I'm not afraid of a bear. If we see one, we'll just make a lot of noise and scare him off."

"What about the Indians?" Amos asked in a low voice.

"We'll just stay out of their way," Clara replied without looking at him.

How? Amos wondered. He'd heard the men talking last night at supper. They had agreed that Indians could read a trail over bare rock as easily as other people read deer tracks in a plowed field. It would be no problem at all for them to follow the path made by three children and a cow.

"Besides," Clara went on, "we're not far from

Marietta. Papa said we'd be there in a couple of days."

"But that was on the water," Amos reminded her. "It'll take a lot longer by land."

Clara leveled an angry gaze on Amos. "It can't be more than three or four days . . . five at the most."

Amos pushed his hands in his pockets and kept silent. Clara seemed to think walking to Marietta was not much more than a stroll across a pasturefield. He hoped it would be that easy, but he had his doubts.

"I'm hungry, Sister." Amos and Clara turned to see Jonathan coming toward them, scratching his head. His beaver hat hung down his back on rawhide strings.

"Jonathan!" Clara burst out. "Queen Anne saved you. I knew she would. She's strong and brave and—"

"She saved me first, then I saved her," Jonathan interrupted. "She had trouble getting up the bank, so I pushed her up. I'm hungry," he repeated.

"So am I," Clara said and reached for her soggy knapsack. She began pulling things into her lap, a blue calico shawl, small bottles of herbs and seeds, a tin cup and spoon, a wooden comb. She cast a quick glance at Amos as she lifted out the long-barreled pistol.

"Where's the food?" Jonathan asked.

"I have some jerky in here somewhere," Clara said. "Here it is." She drew out a thin brown packet and unwound the wet cloth, then held it out to Jonathan and Amos.

For several minutes the three of them chewed on the tough, stringy meat. It looked more like dirty leather than real food, but it was salty and satisfying. Rolling up what was left, Clara laid it aside and brought out a shiny crimson apple. She took a bite, then handed it to Jonathan who bit off a chunk and passed it on to Amos. Taking turns, they reduced the apple to a thin core and a few brown seeds. Clara picked out the seeds and dropped them into one of her herb jars, then nibbled the core away to nothing.

"Can I have another piece of jerky?" Jonathan asked.

"No, not now," Clara said, tucking her few possessions back into the knapsack. "We'll need it later on."

"Are we lost, Sister?"

"Jonathan, just because we're in the woods doesn't mean we're lost," Clara said. "You were never lost in the woods back home."

"No, but that was home," Jonathan murmured. "I wish Papa was here." A shiver rippled over his slim frame like wind across water.

Amos laid a hand on his brother's shoulder, feeling the same yearning, the same raw fear. He could never have imagined that they would be separated from their father and marooned in this wild country. Even worse, they were in Indian territory, with only a few meager strips of jerky to keep them from starving. He looked at Clara, hoping she would know what to do.

She rose to her feet, pulling at her wet, clinging clothes. "We need to get dried out," she said. She untied her apron and hung it over a bush. Loosening the strings of her bodice, she opened it wide to let the sun and wind get to her chemise, an under-blouse made of soft cotton. Then she began wringing the excess water from her ankle-length skirt.

As Amos and Jonathan peeled off their shirts and spread them in the sun, Queen Anne came toward them. She started grazing on the lush grass and didn't even raise her head when Clara knelt and began squeezing milk into the tin cup. Once it was full, Clara handed the brimming cup to Jonathan. He drank it down in one long gulp.

The cup had to be filled several more times before they were all satisfied. Then, knowing there'd be plenty more by evening, Clara squirted milk on the ground until Queen Anne's udder hung limp and empty.

While they waited for their clothes to dry, the three of them talked about the night attack at Wheeling and about their father.

"Papa's all right, isn't he, Sister?" Jonathan said.

"You know Papa," Clara replied in a confident voice. "He can look after himself. He always has his rifle with him."

"I'll bet Papa was more worried about us than he was about himself," Amos said.

Clara nodded. "He's probably looking for us already."

"Then why don't we just wait here," Jonathan said. "If he comes in a boat, we can give a holler."

Amos and Clara exchanged a quick glance before Clara answered. "Jonathan, we're in Indian country and we've got to stay quiet. Our best chance is to go on to Marietta."

"You mean walk all the way to Marietta?" Jonathan asked.

"It's not far," Clara said. "We walked all the way from Lancaster to the Ohio River, didn't we?"

"Yes, but we had Papa then," Jonathan declared.

The three of them sat in silence, each with his own thoughts about the father they'd left behind. One thing they knew for certain; if he was alive, he would come for them. That knowledge, along with the warming sun and the murmuring river, combined to lull their senses and make them drowsy.

Even after Jonathan and Clara had drifted off to sleep, Amos remained awake, trying to figure a way out of their predicament. They were alone in the wilderness, with no food, no way of knowing how far they'd have to travel to reach Marietta. Besides that, there were wild animals and Indians.

Amos had always loved the woods, felt at ease in their cool, dappled shade. In Pennsylvania, where the open woodlands served as pasture for the livestock, a short walk always brought him out of the trees and into plowed fields. But the Ohio forests were unbroken by fields or homesteads, unmarked even by trails. Here the dark, dense edge of the woods was a wall that hemmed them in, crowded them against the river. A few steps away from the Ohio, Amos thought, and they could be hopelessly lost.

If he was alone, it wouldn't matter if he got lost, wouldn't even matter if the Indians found him. In fact, if he went to live with the Indians, he might be able to forget about Simon. But it was different for Clara and Jonathan. They had no haunting memories to escape. Amos hoped that if the Indians should capture them, he would have the courage to make the same kind of bargain Blue Jacket had made. But the thought of being separated from Clara and Jonathan, of never seeing his father again, made him shudder. They'd just have to get to Marietta before the Indians found them.

CHAPTER 4

Amos woke before the others and wandered down to the water's edge. He scanned the river, looking for anything that might signal danger. It was a matter of life and death, his father had said, to see before you were seen.

Sunlight bouncing off the water blinded him and he squeezed his eyes half-shut. Everyone in the family said he had the eyes of an eagle. It was true he saw things that most people missed, but he believed it was because he spent so much time out of doors. Studying the animals and trees and birds, he'd learned to recognize anything that was not as it should be, an odd movement, an alien sound, a color that did not fit.

Upstream, where the river curved out of sight, there was a spot along the far shore, a puzzling shape in the water that he couldn't identify. Just to be safe, he sank to his knees, then parted the reeds for another look. He thought of the trick his Uncle Daniel had taught him when they'd hunted back home, a trick that helped narrow his vision to one small spot. Curling his hand into a fist, he peered with one eye through the spyglass tunnel between his fingers and his palm.

Now he saw it clearly. It was a canoe gliding along in the murky shade, sometimes disappearing where a tree's heavy branches trailed in the water. Two men, one at each end of the canoe, paddled with smooth, cautious strokes, while two others rode low in the center of the craft. Even at this distance, Amos could tell they were Indians.

Amos edged backward until he reached Clara and Jonathan. They were still asleep, and more important, so was Queen Anne. If she should bawl out, the sound would be heard for miles.

He crept back to the river and watched the canoe easing along the opposite shore. The Indians seemed as wary as he was about being seen. Amos wondered if they were some of last night's attackers. He clenched his jaws tight and willed them onward. As they grew smaller with distance, he began to relax, sure that he hadn't been detected.

When the trees on his side of the river obstructed his view, he returned to Clara and Jonathan. While he was slipping on his shirt, Clara stirred and sat up. He told her about the canoe.

"Are they gone?" she asked.

"Yes, but there'll probably be more," Amos said. "From now on, we'd better stay out of sight under the trees."

Clara nodded and leaned over and nudged Jonathan. As he yawned and rubbed his eyes, she reached for her dry clothes. "We might as well start walking. We can get along a piece before dark."

"Do you think we're doing the right thing, going on to Marietta?" Amos asked. It scared him, to think of leaving his father back there, but he'd do what Clara said. He trusted her judgment more than his own.

"Papa knew we were on the boat," Clara replied. "When he finds it gone, he'll think we took it, and he'll look for us downriver."

She was probably right, Amos thought. If they walked along the riverbank, they were bound to get to Marietta sooner or later. He was beginning to understand how people in this territory used the Ohio River. Either they traveled it by boat or they followed its broad, sunlit corridor through the forest. It not only served as a highway, it was also a familiar landmark that told people where they were. Even now, there might be someone nearby, friend or enemy, making his way through the trees, following the river. The thought sent a chill over Amos.

"If the Indians were to capture us . . ." he began.

"I'm not worried about Indians," Clara said. "We got away from them last night, and I expect we can do it again."

Looking at his sister, Amos couldn't help but smile. Nothing frightened her. She had a kind of blustering fearlessness that both thrilled and terrified him. A fellow couldn't tell what she might do. He sometimes thought that if they should meet a real, woods-wild Indian, Clara would probably march right up to him and declare she was taking him prisoner.

Once they were all dressed, they headed downriver. Sunlight slanted over Amos's left shoulder at first, but as they moved into the trees, the light dimmed to a soft, green glow. In the hushed quiet, they spoke in whispers. There was no underbrush, only moss-covered logs and feathery ferns and a spongy carpet of dead leaves. Black hardwood trunks soared into the dense, leafy umbrella that shut out the sun. His father had been right about the trees. They were giants.

Walking in the semi-darkness, it seemed to Amos that the whole world had gone green. He longed for the sun and his gaze turned often in the direction of the river. Occasional glimpses of light on the water made him breathe easier.

The day was dying when the forest gave way to open sky. They squinted, half-blind, at the sight before them. Hundreds of fallen trees littered the ground, piled up in some places as high as houses. New trees had sprung up between the dead logs, but they were not yet mature enough to close out the sun.

"It must have taken a monstrous wind to do all that damage," Amos remarked.

"How are we going to get over the logs?" Jonathan asked.

Clara stood with an arm around the Jersey's neck. "We can cut inland a ways," she suggested, "then swing back to the river."

"But what if we can't find the river again?" Jonathan protested.

"We're not going to be far from it. Look, you can see the edge of the woods from here." Clara pointed away from the river to where the jumbled dead trees merged into the living forest.

"Jonathan's right. If we lose sight of the river, we'll be lost," Amos warned.

Clara gazed at him a moment, her eyes clouded with thought. "If you're worried about getting lost,

I'll take Queen Anne and go around the logs," she said, "while you two climb over them. You keep an eye on the river, Amos, and Jonathan can walk between us where he can see you and me both."

Clara's plan sounded as if it would work, so Amos nodded agreement. When she went off with the cow in tow, he and Jonathan began their difficult crossing. As Amos struggled over and through the morass of rotting logs, his gaze swung like a pendulum from the river's sparkle to Jonathan's big hat, and back to the river again. He couldn't see Clara but he hoped Jonathan was keeping her in sight.

By the time he'd reached the other side of the windfall, Amos was thirsty and wet with sweat. He leaned against a live tree, waiting. Jonathan soon appeared, then Clara with Queen Anne plodding along behind.

"Let's stop here for the night," Clara said, sinking down on the ground. "I'm hungry and tired, and I don't think I can walk anymore." She started digging in her knapsack.

It took only minutes for the three of them to finish off the last few strips of jerky. They washed it down with warm milk. There was plenty of that, and when they'd had enough, Clara milked the rest out onto the ground.

As a quiet twilight stole through the woods,

Amos watched the river's half-hidden light change from red to pink to fading gray. He hoped the river would reflect the stars when they came out.

As they were piling up leaves for a bed, they heard a faint rumble from the west.

"Sounds like we'll get rain before morning," Amos said with a sigh. There'd be no stars overhead or in the river.

"This maple will keep us dry," Clara said. "You remember the sugar tree in the corner of the yard back home? Remember how we used to climb up in it and . . ."

"I wish we were still there," Jonathan interrupted. Then in a softer voice he added, "I wish Papa was here."

Clara glanced at Amos, then back at Jonathan. "Papa'll find us, or else we'll find him in Marietta. We just have to get there."

Amos's spirits sank as he thought of his father. Clara talked as if he was all right, but what if he'd been wounded in the attack . . . or worse? Recalling the night raid on Wheeling, Amos relived the noise, the confusion, the dreaded sound of guns. Memories of Simon rose unbidden then, making the night come close and dark.

He reached for the sack of marbles at his waist, swallowing hard as he felt Simon's favorite agate shooter. These past months, the big green marble had been both a comfort and a curse. He'd won it the day before the accident, meaning to keep it for a couple of days, then let Simon win it back. But before he'd thought of it again, Simon was dead. Several times he'd considered throwing it away, but he just couldn't do it. Now it was like a hot coal that burned him whenever he held it. He let go of the marble pouch and lay down, hoping he wouldn't dream of Simon.

The sound of splattering raindrops woke Amos, and seconds later the storm descended. He put his hands over his ears to soften the thunder's boom. Lightning forked across the sky and in its bold light, he saw Clara and Jonathan sitting upright, staring into the downpour. They'd endured storms coming from Pennsylvania, sometimes remaining dry under a tree's thick foliage. But the maple tree was no match for this storm. They were soon soaked.

As the night passed, they huddled against Queen Anne, gathering both heat and cheer from her solid, warm bulk. Finally, the landscape took form in the pale light preceding sunrise and the rain slowed to a quiet drizzle.

"I wish we had a fire so we could get warm," Jonathan said, shivering.

Clara rummaged in her knapsack for several moments, then turned to Amos. "Do you have a flint and steel?"

Amos shook his head. He'd had no need for fire-making tools on the trail because their father always carried flint and steel in his pocket. With a little dry tinder, he could have a fire going in a few minutes.

"I'm hungry," Jonathan said.

"Even if we could catch some game," Clara said, "we don't have a fire to cook it, and I'm certainly not going to eat raw meat. But we've got plenty of milk," she added, pulling out her tin cup. They drank as much as they could hold while the patient Jersey nibbled at a mossy log.

As they entered the woods again, Amos gazed back with longing at the windfall and the low clouds overhead. They might not stand under open sky again for days. Rain worked through the high, layered canopy and dripped on them. There was hardly a sound of their passing from the wet leaves.

Jonathan was leading the way when he let out a yelp and fell backwards over a fallen log. Amos rushed forward, terrified that he'd come face to face with a bear, or worse yet, Indians. Instead, he saw a startled tom turkey, feathers ruffled, wings fluttering. For a few seconds, the frightened bird stood his ground; then he turned and fled, a blur of brown along the forest floor.

"I'd like to have had him on a spit," Clara said.

"I would, too," Amos said. "Why didn't you grab him, Jonathan?" He grinned, knowing that capturing a wild turkey by hand was harder than catching a handful of smoke.

Some time later, they came across a tiny stream rippling toward the Ohio. As Queen Anne drank her fill, Clara followed the stream's course to the riverbank. Fed by some distant spring, the stream had created a sandbar that ran out through a shaded cove and into the river. Just then, the sun came out, bathing the sandbar in warm, yellow light.

"Let's go down there," Clara said. "We can get our clothes dry." Without waiting for the boys, she led Queen Anne down the bank and out onto the sandy beach. The boys followed, pausing to study a five-toed animal track at the water's edge.

While Clara and Jonathan chased minnows through the shallows, Amos wandered along the sunny sandbar. The bright, glittering water blinded him, but the sun's warmth was as comforting as a downy quilt on a winter's night. He watched a gathering of Carolina parakeets fluttering among the trees downstream. Their yellow and orange heads glared brightly against the foliage. If there were Indians about, he reasoned, the birds would have squawked and taken flight. He relaxed a little and gazed across at the Virginia shore. Someone could be watching from those black shadows, but it was worth the risk to spend a few minutes in the sun.

The sandbar reached out beyond the shoreline and Amos walked to its very end to get a view of the whole river. As he gazed upstream, his breath caught in his throat. He could scarcely believe what he saw. There was a flatboat coming toward him, its new lumber bright against the gray water.

"Clara, come quick! There's a boat," he called, never taking his eyes off the approaching craft.

Clara and Jonathan ran over to him, and stared with open mouths at the boat bearing down on them. It looked much like the one they'd traveled on, the frame of squared timbers, with a cabin in the middle and a livestock pen on the stern deck. There were people scattered around the boat, women sitting on crates, men studying the riverbanks, children playing on the cabin roof.

"We're saved!" Clara exclaimed. "They can't miss us. We won't have to walk to Marietta after all, Jonathan." He grinned at her and they began hollering and waving their arms.

A man on the boat's cabin roof pointed in their

direction and soon everyone on the boat was staring at them.

"They've seen us," Amos announced. Now, with the certain knowledge of their rescue at hand, he wondered if there were Indians nearby who could have heard their shouts. Then he dismissed that worry. They would be on the boat in a few minutes and safe from any danger on shore.

As the boat came closer, Amos noticed several men huddled at the bow, talking, gesturing toward the sandbar. All of a sudden, the group scattered. Two men jumped to the oars while the other men, one by one, returned to the boat railing with rifles in their hands. Amos felt a cold pain in his stomach. He knew they weren't going to stop, even before he saw the boat veering gently but surely away toward the south shore.

"No!" Clara's voice rose from a moan to a scream. "No. Come and get us. We're stranded here. Help us!" The people in the boat stood staring across the water like cold, unfeeling statues. She turned to Amos in disbelief. "They're not coming!"

Amos shook his head, then gazed again at the receding boat. He'd already figured out why they didn't stop. They were afraid. They'd been warned that Indians sometimes used prisoners to lure a boat close to shore and then attack it. Though three children and a cow might look harmless enough, they couldn't take the chance.

The boat passed downriver, and moments later, floated around a bend and out of sight. Clara bent and picked up a handful of stones and hurled them with all her might out into the river. "There was plenty of room for us—they're mean and . . . don't they have any feelings for—"

"What are we going to do now, Sister?" Jonathan asked, his voice cracking. For once, Clara had no ready response.

Amos stared at the spot where the boat had disappeared. It was no use hoping for rescue. If other boats came downriver, none of them would stop. We won't find any help on this side of the river either, Amos thought. The only people here are Indians. The thought of Indians stirred him to action.

"Come on. We've got to get away from the river," he said.

"What are you talking about?" Clara countered, her eyes still blazing.

"Indians," Amos replied. "They may have heard us. We've got to get back in the trees." He forgot for the moment that he never told Clara what to do, but he remembered his father's warning: "There are always Indians." He scrambled up the bank and into the refuge of the forest.

Clara glared once more at the bend of the river, then followed him without any further mention of the flatboat. It had entered and exited their lives so quickly that it seemed to have been only a dream.

CHAPTER 5

~~~~~~

They scaled the riverbank and moved into a grove of towering oaks. Tree trunks rose like giant black candles from the forest floor and vanished into the dense foliage overhead. The open woods made easy walking, but it also left them exposed. Amos knew that even if they should see an Indian before he saw them, it wouldn't make much difference. There was no place to hide.

"Slow down, Amos," Clara called.

He stopped and waited for her and Jonathan. "We need to get as far from here as we can before dark," he told her.

"They'd never be able to track us through these trees," Clara said. She pointed back along the ground she'd just covered. "You can't even see where we walked."

"I can't, but I'll bet an Indian could," Amos said.

"I'm hungry," Jonathan said, sagging to the ground.

Amos thought of the jerky they'd had the night before. The few meager strips had barely dulled their hunger. There were plenty of animal signs in the woods, and sounds of them fleeing the human intruders, but there was no way to catch any of them. Squirrels scolded them from above with a mocking chatter. We're lucky to have Queen Anne's milk, Amos thought, but what we need is meat.

As if reading his thoughts, Clara spoke up. "We've got to get something solid to eat, Amos. We can't walk if we don't have the strength. I wish I had a cooking pot. I saw some nettles back there by—"

"I don't want any nettles," Jonathan announced. "They taste like spinach."

"When you get honest-to-Jacob hungry," Clara said, "you'll eat anything."

"I'm already honest-to-Jacob hungry," Jonathan replied, "but I don't like spinach."

Amos didn't bother to point out that even if they had a cooking pot, they didn't have any fire. "Maybe we'll come across a walnut tree," he said, "or a hickory. Papa said there were plenty of nut trees out here."

He should have been looking, he thought, because every hour that passed, they got hungrier and weaker. He recalled the hot skillet bread they'd had for supper on Wheeling Island and the memory of it made his mouth water. It could be a long time before they tasted bread again.

"There's no use sitting here talking about food when we don't have any," Clara said. Assuming command again, she walked off with Queen Anne.

Amos was content to let her lead, but he kept himself alert for any visible signs of humans or sounds that might signal danger. The woods were as dim and cool and quiet as a cellar.

They had walked for some time when Amos noticed that the forest seemed brighter. Maybe they were coming to another clearing. Ahead, thin shafts of sunlight reached the ground, allowing bushes and seedling trees to thrive. He heard Clara's loud sigh and when he stopped beside her, he expelled his breath, too. A good-sized creek lay across their path. Its banks fell at least twenty feet straight down, bare and slick with mud. The creek was a tributary of the Ohio, but Amos knew it was much more than that. It was an impassable rift that lay between them and Marietta.

"We can't get across that," Jonathan said.

"The banks are too steep," Amos agreed. "We

could slide down into the water, but we'd never get up the other side."

"Even if we could, Queen Anne couldn't," Clara said. The Jersey, oblivious to their predicament, chomped at the tender grass along the bank.

Finally Clara spoke again. "We'll just have to go along this side until we find a spot to cross. We'll be leaving the Ohio, but this stream will always lead us back to it. There's nothing else . . ."

"I'm tired of walking," Jonathan mumbled and dropped down on the ground.

"Get up, Jonathan," Clara ordered. "We're going to keep walking until we get to Marietta, no matter how far it is." She prodded him to his feet. "I know you're hungry. We all are. But we have to keep—"

"All right, Sister, but what do we do when we can't walk any more . . . crawl?"

Clara grinned and slapped his shoulder. "I'll crawl and you can ride on my back," she said.

Coaxing the reluctant cow from her grazing, they started upstream. Food was never far from Amos's thoughts now. His whole body cried out for nourishment. Each step seemed to require more and more effort, and sometimes he stumbled in the wet leaves. This detour was making them use up what little strength they had left. I'd give anything for a bite of meat, he thought, licking his lips.

Though the creek gradually narrowed, the bank remained hopelessly steep. Once Amos spied a chestnut tree on the opposite bank and was angry that he couldn't get to it. He'd be sure to watch for it when they went back downstream.

Just then, Clara exclaimed and dropped to the ground. Where sunlight warmed the creek bank, wild strawberries had taken root and now yielded fruit. They crawled around on their hands and knees to find every precious berry, even gulping down some that were still green.

The berries, along with the brief stop, refreshed them and gave them the will to continue. Amos was leading the way when he looked down into the creek bed and saw the riffle. A shoal of sand and small stones clogged the streambed and channeled the water to one side where it flowed only inches deep. It was what they'd been looking for, a place with low banks and shallow water.

As Amos scrambled down to the riffle, he watched a silvery fish flash from the shallows into deep water. If only they had a hook and line.

"Do you have any fishhooks in your knapsack?" he asked Clara as she led Queen Anne down the bank.

"No, they were in the chest on the boat."

"There ought to be some way to catch a fish," Amos said.

"Could you eat it raw?" Clara asked, wrinkling her nose.

"I forgot," Amos mumbled, feeling his hope, like the creek's quiet flow, ebbing away. Maybe the time would come when he got hungry enough to eat raw fish. But not yet.

The easy crossing lifted their spirits and they headed back toward the Ohio at a livelier pace. Amos had forgotten the Indians in his eager search for food. He had to find that chestnut tree. His eyes on the overhead branches, he yelped when his bare foot came down on a chestnut burr. The ground was covered with them, prickly, brown pods opened by last fall's prying frosts. He heard a barking sound over his head and located the squirrel by its angry, snapping tail. He pointed to the few chestnuts still clinging intact to the branches. Somehow, they had escaped the winter and the greedy squirrels.

"I'll climb up and get them," Jonathan said, not waiting for anyone's consent.

Amos watched his brother clamber up the trunk and out onto a sturdy limb, whistling as he went. He was as sure-footed as the squirrel, Amos thought, and almost as noisy.

Jonathan dropped nuts from above while Clara and Amos set to work, pounding apart the bristled pods between stones, then cracking open the thin inner shells. Half-moon kernels, as big as the end of a man's thumb, came out in one piece.

On the ground again, Jonathan tossed a nut into his mouth. "Finally, we've got something to chew."

"You'd better go easy," Amos warned him, "or you'll end up with a complaining stomach."

"I'm saving some of these for later," Clara said, dropping a handful of uncracked nuts into her knapsack.

Amos stuffed a few in his pocket. "I wish we had a fire. They'd be much better roasted," he said.

"They're good anyway," Jonathan said around a mouthful.

"Are you sure you got them all?" Amos asked, tossing a spiny casing at his brother. When it stuck in Jonathan's hair, he pulled it out and threw it back at Amos. Soon chestnut burrs were flying through the air, as thick as swarming bees. Jonathan yelped when a well-aimed burr hit him in the nose.

"Sassafras!" Clara hissed. "You'll have the whole Indian nation down on us. Come on, Queen Anne, you and I are going to Marietta. Those knot-headed boys can just stay here and fuss until the Indians find them." She stalked away, still grumbling, while the cow kept turning her head to look at the rowdy boys they were leaving behind. In only moments, Amos and Jonathan had caught up.

By the time they reached the spot where the stream emptied into the Ohio, dusk had descended. The river, fast losing the light, shone like molten lead. Choosing a clear, mossy place under an oak tree for their night camp, Amos and Jonathan sprawled on the ground while Clara milked the cow. Warm milk and the few saved nuts served as their supper.

"How far do you think we've come?" Amos asked Clara. In the dark he could barely see her face.

"Only three or four miles downriver, I'd guess," Clara replied. "This walk to Marietta is going to take longer than I thought, with the creek in our way and—"

"We should just stay here by the river," Jonathan said. "Papa can find us."

"We've got to keep going, as long as . . ." Clara's voice trailed off and she glanced at Amos, then away.

As long as we're able, Amos thought. Even now, he could feel his stomach twisting in upon itself. The cow's milk brought only temporary relief and the nuts were all gone. If they didn't get something to eat soon, something substantial, there could come a time when they wouldn't have the strength to go on.

Sometime during the night, Amos awoke and sat

up. He wasn't sure what had roused him, maybe a night bird, or an animal creeping over the dead leaves. Though it was dark under the trees, a swath of moonlight slashed the surface of the river like a glittering silver sword.

Amos lifted his head and inhaled a long breath. Now he knew what had wakened him. Smoke! Carried on the night wind, it was barely noticeable, but there was no mistaking the pungent odor. He made a complete circle, looking for a light or a glow in the sky. The darkness was deep and unbroken.

He rose to his feet and took a few steps away from the camp. Fire meant danger, whether natural or man-made. The woods could be burning, and the fire could be coming their way. If it wasn't a forest fire, then the smoke meant other humans were somewhere near. He'd better walk out a ways and investigate before he woke Clara and Jonathan. No need for them to worry too.

Using his nose as a guide and the moonlit river as a beacon, he set off downstream. An owl hooted in the distance and a large animal crashed away through the woods to his right. A deer, he guessed, from the sound of it.

His thoughts slipped back to Pennsylvania, to a night last spring when he and Simon and his cousin Ethan had camped in the woods. They'd built a fire to cook the rabbit Ethan had shot. Stretched out by the blazing logs, they'd been amazed when a fawn staggered into the firelight. It stood frozen in place, staring at them with gleaming, startled eyes, then as suddenly as it had appeared, it was gone. Simon had spoken then, and in memory Amos could still hear his voice. "Animals have feelings too," Simon had said, and Amos and Ethan had nodded their agreement. It was one of those times when everything in the world seemed right.

Amos swiped a hand across his eyes, knowing this was not the time to think of Simon. Just then, he stumbled over a log and fell forward into a clump of brush, making as much noise as the deer he'd flushed earlier. He proceeded with more caution, groping his way. The moon-washed river was a reassuring sight in the darkness and as long as he kept it in sight, he knew he'd have no trouble finding his way back to camp.

The land lifted for a ways, then leveled off. Just in time, he saw the telltale glow below him. He sank to his knees and his heart seemed to stop beating. The dying fire cast flickering shadows over a group of Indians.

CHAPTER 6

Amos eased down on his stomach with a cold knot clogging his throat like an unswallowed chunk of food. Hands clenched beneath his chin, he stared down into the dusky ravine. The Indians had chosen their campsite well. It was near the Ohio, but a low knoll hid their fire from enemy eyes on the river.

The Indians were huddled around the fire, speaking in low tones that floated up to Amos like faraway thunder. As they talked, they pulled pieces of meat from two skinned animals suspended over the fire. Squirrel, Amos guessed. His mouth watered, imagining the taste of the hot, juicy meat. The Indians gnawed the bones, then tossed the remains into the nearby brush.

Amos counted seven in all. Just then, one of the men stood up, his chin lifted, his body as rigid as a tree trunk. Amos held his breath and listened, too, but he couldn't hear anything unusual. Only a few moments passed before a tall Indian carrying a rifle stepped out of the shadows and squatted by the fire. Now there were eight.

Amos shivered, wondering if there were any more Indians out there in the darkness. Even though he made no noise, they still might stumble onto his hiding place. He dropped his forehead on his hands. He had to get away from here, and soon. Daylight could be only minutes away. When the men went to sleep, he would be able to escape . . . if he was careful and quiet. He breathed a silent sigh of relief as he saw the Indians stretching out by the fire. Now all he had to do was be patient.

Amos waited, his eyes growing heavy in the darkness. He thought of Clara and Jonathan. If they woke and found him gone, they'd be worried sick, and scared. He wished now he'd never decided to investigate the smoke.

Gazing down at the campsite, he stiffened when he saw that one Indian was not sleeping. The man's lean form blended into the darkness, almost invisible beside a tree. Amos stared at the spot, blinking his tired eyes, straining to see, but the shadows blurred into inky blackness. Moments later, he was shocked to see the Indian leaning against a tree on the opposite side of the fire. If the man could move without being seen or heard, Amos was in grave danger.

Now he was more afraid to go than to stay. Any movement he made was sure to be heard by the stealthy sentinel below. As much as he wanted to, he couldn't risk sleeping either. He'd just have to remain still and hope the Indians would leave when morning came.

A damp cold crept up from the ground and chilled Amos's bones. Mosquitoes swarmed around him and his only protection was to bury his face in his arms. Even then, they buzzed and bit his ears until he felt like screaming. He shifted his body to ward them off, but when the leaves rustled under him, he froze. There was nothing to do but let them bite. He wondered if mosquitoes were biting the sleeping Indians. He hoped so and the thought brought him some satisfaction.

Just when he was sure he couldn't endure another minute of the torture, Amos realized that the weeds in front of his face had paled from black to gray-green. Day was coming. He watched the campsite take shape in the smoky, gray light.

As if anxious that they should be up before the sun, the camp guard began nudging the feet of the sleeping men. One minute they were there, rising, stretching, rubbing their eyes like sleepy children, the next minute they were gone.

Amos stared down into the empty ravine. Only smoking logs remained to tell that anyone had ever been there. For several minutes he forced himself to stay hidden and still. When he felt sure the Indians were not returning and were probably far away by now, he stood up. Flexing his stiff arms and legs, he gazed around.

He couldn't be sure how far he'd come in the night, but he knew the Ohio lay off to his left, and its mist-shrouded trail would lead him straight back to Clara and Jonathan.

He wrapped his arms around his chilled body and gazed down at the Indian camp. Scattered logs still smoldered, giving off a wispy smoke. There was bound to be some heat in them, he thought. He sprang forward, slipping and sliding down the leaf-covered slope. One of the logs was charred black and still warm, but there was no spark. He found a shorter log that glowed red when he rolled it over. Now he had the makings of a fire.

He gathered some dry grass and fed the smoldering embers. Blowing gently, then laying on more tinder, he soon had a tiny blaze. He rolled several of the half-burned logs together, feeling his spirits rise with the leaping flames.

As he knelt and warmed himself, a thrilling idea flashed in Amos's mind. He could take the fire back to Clara and Jonathan, if he could figure out how to carry it.

For a moment he thought of the Indians. He'd located them by tracing the smoke from their fire. He knew he could be found the same way, but he'd have to take the risk. They needed some real cooked food if they were going to get to Marietta.

On the side of the ravine where light cut through the trees, Amos spied a patch of blackberry bushes. He could use the stalks to make a basket for carrying the fire. They would be thin and pliant, and he could cut off the thorns with his knife. Scrambling up the hill, he cut a dozen or so of the wiry branches and carried them back to the fire.

After slicing away the needle-sharp thorns, he began weaving a loose basket. It turned out flat, like a mat, but when he gathered the stalk ends together, he had a shallow pocket for the fire. Using his knife and a stick, he maneuvered several of the burning logs into the carrier. Amos felt a kind of trembling excitement when he thought of returning to camp with his prize. He was taking Clara and Jonathan something they wanted now more than anything else in the world. Following the smoke had been a good idea after all, he decided.

As he got up to leave, he noticed smoke curling out of the fire basket. The blackberry stalks were smoldering and would soon burn through unless he put something between them and the fire. He dumped the logs out onto the ground. That was it! Soil wouldn't burn, and a little tinder underneath the logs would keep them ablaze until he got back to camp.

Amos used his knife to cut out a square of sod. As he laid it in the basket, an odd-looking stick fell out on the ground. But it wasn't a stick. It was a bone, one that an Indian had gnawed clean and thrown away.

He picked it up and sniffed it. Though there was no meat left on it, the smell of cooked meat lingered. He put it between his teeth and bit into it. It tasted bland and dry, but somehow satisfying. When he broke through to the bone's center, he sucked out the soft, sweet marrow. The Indians couldn't have been very hungry, to ignore all that goodness.

Amos searched for more of the discarded bones and soon had a handful, resolving to take some back to Clara and Jonathan. He grinned to himself, wondering what Clara would think about eating second-hand bones.

When he arrived at the campsite, Clara and Jonathan were still asleep. As quietly as he could,

Amos dumped out the smoldering logs and set about making a real fire. This spot, barely hidden from the river, was all right for a daytime fire, but he knew they'd have to camp away from the river when night fell.

If only they had some kind of meat to cook. He noticed the cow nibbling at a clump of grass. She wasn't suffering from hunger. Her body was rounded and full, and her healthy brown coat shone in the morning light. He recalled the times they had butchered cattle for meat back in Pennsylvania. Clara would be mad as a hornet if she guessed what he was thinking. But Amos knew he couldn't harm Queen Anne, even if he was starving. She was like a member of the family. Besides, her milk had gotten them this far.

The snapping, crackling blaze woke Clara first. She stared at the fire, balled her fists into her eyes, then stared again. "Where did you . . . how did you . . . ?"

Jonathan sat up, then grinned as he scrambled over and held out his hands to the flames.

Amos told them of the Indians and his night of hiding. The red welts on his face and arms were clear proof of what he had endured.

Clara gave him little sympathy. "It was worth it," she said, jumping to her feet. "We've got fire now.

The next thing to do is find something to cook over it. If I only had a pot . . . ."

Amos remembered the meatless bones he'd collected. "I've got something else," he said, emptying his pocket and handing Clara and Jonathan each a bone, then taking one for himself.

"Where'd you get these?" Clara asked, holding the bare bone at arm's length.

"At the Indian camp," Amos told her. "Don't ask any questions, just eat."

Clara sniffed at it, brushed off a few grains of dirt, then began nibbling.

"I'll bet I can catch a frog," Jonathan said, cracking the bone between his teeth.

Amos stared at Jonathan and an image of another time edged into his mind. He and Simon had often gone to Meller's pond to catch the giant bullfrogs that thrived among the reeds. They'd roasted the meaty hind legs over an evening fire and listened to the thrumming, bass sounds of the old wily frogs that had gotten away.

"Do you, Amos?" Jonathan was asking.

"What?" Amos looked up, letting the painful memory drift off into a corner of his mind.

"Do you think you and me could catch some frogs?" Jonathan repeated.

"Sure," Amos replied, rising to his feet. "And I

might be able to spear a fish, too. Let's go see what we can find for breakfast." As they walked away, Amos called back to Clara. "Keep the fire going."

He and Jonathan worked their way along the bank to where the creek emptied into the Ohio. Logs and other debris washed down by the spring floods had lodged on a sandbar, creating a quiet backwater.

"I'll bet there's frogs in there," Jonathan said and waded into the shade-blackened water.

"Watch out for snakes," Amos said, "and if you see a fish in the shallows, dive on it. I'm going to find a piece of oak to make a spear. I'll be back in a while. Remember, no hollering, no matter how big the frog is."

Jonathan was already stalking a bug-eyed frog, his beaver hat pulled low over his eyes.

Amos found an oak tree and broke off a slender branch. After stripping it of leaves, he began whittling one end down to a sharp point. There must be plenty of fish in the creek, he thought, and if he was quick enough, they'd have real food for a change. If Jonathan caught a frog or two, they'd have a feast.

Amos could see the glint of sunlit water. He worked his way through the trees until he stood on the bank of the Ohio. The river and the distant shore glowed in peaceful emptiness. It could have been a river back in Pennsylvania, except that over the solitude hovered the nagging knowledge of danger.

Tired from his nighttime escapade, Amos dropped down among the weeds to rest. But as he continued to work on the wooden spear, he kept an eye on the river. This was no place to be careless. He squinted upstream at a brushy island shimmering in the sun close by the Virginia shore. Lifting a hand to shield his eyes, he studied the open water.

Something bobbed on the surface between him and the island. The object dissolved in the sparkling water, came into view again, then vanished. Just when he thought it was gone for good, it reappeared. The current carried it along, sometimes lifting it higher in the water, sometimes washing over it. It was probably a log, he reasoned, but there was something about its shape that held his attention.

On a sudden rising surge, the object skimmed directly toward him and Amos sucked in his breath. It was a log, but a brown arm was draped over it, and a head rode low in the water beside it. As the log and its clinging passenger came closer, Amos could tell from the black hair and leather-brown skin that it was an Indian.

Even as he edged back into the weeds, Amos

realized that there was no need to hide. He'd already been seen. Black eyes stared at him across the water, not the cold, hostile glare of a warrior but the searing gaze of a person in anguish. Those eyes reminded him of Simon. There was the same look of frightened suffering, the same helpless pleading he'd seen in Simon's eyes the day before he died. Although Amos understood the silent plea, he didn't know what to do.

Just then, the Indian's feet must have touched bottom because he let go of the log. Still staring at Amos, he tried to stand up. Amos could read in his face the terrible longing to reach shore, but there came the moment when the Indian knew he would not succeed. Amos witnessed his silent surrender to the river. Moments later, water closed over the sinking head.

Amos stared at the spot, his breath choking him, just as he imagined the Indian must be choking for lack of air. The river would pull him down and down into its murky depths until he drowned. The image drove Amos to action. He threw aside his knife and spear and jumped into the water. The river's pull was powerful as the water rose to his waist, then his shoulders. He'd have to be careful or he'd drown, too.

Just in front of him, a brown hand floated to the

surface. He grabbed it and turned for shore. The hand felt cold and lifeless but he clung to it, pulling hard, letting the water carry the load of the body. In the shallow water, he grabbed the Indian under his arms and dragged him up on the bank.

Amos knelt beside the prone figure, watching for signs of life. At last the brown shoulders lifted, and the Indian drew in a shuddering breath. Thinking to make his breathing easier, Amos rolled him onto his back. He was just a boy, maybe a couple of years older than Amos. He wore deerskin leggings, a breechcloth, and knee-high moccasins. Around his neck hung a small leather pouch.

A hole in the boy's leggings caught Amos's eye. Leaning closer, he saw a jagged tear in the boy's thigh, wrinkled and white from the cold water. As bright red blood oozed out and ran down to the ground, Amos rocked back on his heels. There was no mistaking the look of a bullet wound.

CHAPTER 7

$\approx\approx\approx\approx\approx\approx\approx\approx\approx\approx\approx\approx$

The wound brought memories of Simon rushing back. Amos swiped a hand across his eyes, willing his stomach to stop churning. This was no time to relive the nightmare.

He clasped his hands and stared at the still figure on the ground. The boy's eyes were closed and skin stretched tight over his cheekbones gave him a gaunt, half-starved look. The only sign of life was the slow rise and fall of the brown chest.

What could have happened, Amos wondered, to force the boy into the river with such a wound? Surely he wasn't alone. Amos stared out over the Ohio. There could be other Indians searching for the boy right now, but the deserted river reassured him. They couldn't follow a trail through water.

Though the boy's presence meant danger, Amos

wasn't afraid of him. He might be an Indian, but for the moment he was helpless.

The boy's right hand jerked upward, then fluttered back to his chest like a dead leaf falling to the ground. He must be unconscious, Amos decided, maybe close to dying, and the thought brought him to his feet. Clara would know what to do. She'd doctored the whole family for years. He retrieved his knife, then went on the run for Jonathan.

Amos found him crouching at the water's edge. A bulge in his trousers pocket told Amos that he'd caught at least one frog.

"Come quick, Jonathan. I pulled an Indian out of the river and he's hurt bad."

"An Indian!" Jonathan's eyes grew wide.

"Don't worry. He can't hurt us." With a wave of his hand, he urged Jonathan to hurry. "We've got to get him back to Clara."

Jonathan followed Amos, protesting that the two of them couldn't carry a man.

"He's not a man. He's just a boy," Amos said. "And a skinny one, too."

The Indian boy lay as Amos had left him. He looked as if he were sleeping, but the steady stream of blood told the real story.

"What's wrong with him?" Jonathan asked, still

some distance off. He circled the boy, his curiosity battling with his fear.

"He's been shot," Amos said. "I'll take his shoulders and you carry his legs." When Jonathan did not come any closer, Amos glared at him. "Get over here and take a hold of him." The tone of Amos's voice made Jonathan move.

As Amos slid his hands under the limp shoulders, the boy moaned. The wound must hurt like hell's fires, Amos thought, but they had to carry him whether it hurt or not. After struggling up the bank, they laid the boy down to catch their breath. Once they picked him up again, they kept going until they reached Clara.

She was adding wood to the fire when she heard them and spun around. Her mouth fell open and her jaw worked up and down, but no words came out. Even when they laid the boy down, she remained speechless.

"He's hurt real bad," Amos said to her. "He's shot in the thigh. I think the bullet must still be in there."

Clara finally found her voice. "Where did he come from?"

"From the river. He was clear underwater when I grabbed him."

"Whatever possessed you to pull an Indian out of the river?"

"He couldn't make it to shore. He was hanging onto a log and—"

"But an *Indian!*"

"He was real close before I saw he was an Indian. Besides, he needed help. Wouldn't you help a person who was drowning?"

"But he's just a savage!"

Amos looked down at the boy lying as still and limp as a sleeping kitten. Though Clara called him a savage, Amos didn't see anything threatening about him. He was just a boy.

"Clara, you're the only one who can save him. You know what to do for a gunshot wound. You helped with . . ." The rest of the sentence seemed to stick in Amos's throat and wouldn't come out. Anyway, Clara knew what he meant. She'd helped take care of Simon, sat through the night with him, treated him with some of her own herbs.

"Why should we help him?" Clara demanded. "Do you think he would've pulled you out of the river if you'd been drowning?" She stood with her hands on her hips, her eyes flashing fire.

There wasn't time to argue. Amos knelt by the boy and started to pull away the blood-soaked deerskin. Only seconds passed before Clara was at his side.

"All right," she growled. "I'll do what I can, but I

never thought I'd be asked to doctor an Indian. Give me your knife."

She cut away the leather and exposed the raw wound. "He's probably lost a lot of blood. The bullet will have to come out before we can stop the bleeding." She went to get her knapsack hanging in a tree. "I have some dried chickweed I can use for a poultice. I wish I had some comfrey leaves. They're real good for a fresh wound."

She knelt and spread out her blue shawl, then stopped and looked up at the boys. "I need some water," she said, holding out the cup. Jonathan took it and ran toward the creek.

"You'd better get some beech leaves, Amos. I'll make a hot bath to clean the wound."

At that moment, Amos felt a great, swelling admiration for Clara. Not only had she consented to help the Indian, but she knew exactly what to do and what she needed. The boy would never know how lucky he'd been to have Clara for a doctor.

When Amos returned a few minutes later, he saw his knife propped in the red coals and water boiling in the cup. Clara took the beech leaves and dropped several into the hot water, then pulled the cup out of the fire and covered it with a stone. While the beech tea steeped, she tore several pieces of cloth from her petticoat. On one of them, she shook out some of the chickweed and crushed it between her fingers.

"If I'd known I'd be treating a bullet wound," she said, "I'd have been watching for some plantain and willow and such."

"There's plenty of willows down by the river," Jonathan said.

"I'll probably need some bark later," Clara replied. "Amos, come and hold your Indian's legs. I want to see if I can get to the bullet."

Amos knelt and grasped the Indian's legs just above his knees. The skin was cold to his touch, but Amos wasn't surprised. No telling how long the boy had been in the river.

Clara picked up the hot knife, waving it through the air to cool it. The moment she touched the wound, the boy stirred and lashed out with his arms.

"Jonathan, you'll have to hold his hands out of my way," she said.

A deathly quiet reigned as Clara went about her gruesome task. The Indian's weak moans, reminding Amos more of a whimpering puppy than a person, didn't seem to bother Clara at all. With grim concentration, she probed until she found the piece of lead and worked it out of the wound. Laying it aside, she set about bathing the ugly hole with hot beech water. Then, sprinkling a few drops of water onto the chickweed, she blended it into a coarse paste and spread the mixture over the wound. Finally she covered it with a dry cloth.

Amos breathed a sigh of satisfaction as he watched. She has a wondrous, gentle touch when she's doctoring, he thought.

"That's all I know to do," Clara said, and the three of them moved over to the fire.

"I need the knife to clean my frogs," Jonathan said.

"You'd better wash it real good before you start cutting up food," Clara told him. "Scrub it with sand."

As Jonathan headed for the water, Clara scolded Amos. "You could've drowned, you know, trying to save that Indian."

Amos shrugged and stretched his legs toward the fire. His body felt as heavy as a wagonload of bricks. In addition to the lack of sleep, his stomach cried for food. He glanced over at the Indian. They didn't have food for themselves, and now the Indian would need food too, if he lived.

A few minutes later, Jonathan returned with the skinned frog meat skewered on a stick. He sat down and held the meat over the fire. "There's plenty of frogs down there," he said, "if we could only catch them. What we need is a frog gig."

"We'll make one after I rest awhile," Amos said.

"Amos, what are we going to do with the Indian?" Clara asked. When Amos did not answer at once, she went on. "When you pulled that savage out of the river, you tied a millstone around our necks. We can't stay here and look after him. We've got to get to Marietta."

"We can't leave him here to die," Amos said.

"Sassafras, Amos, he's just an Indian! Anyway, I think the bleeding has stopped. If the wound doesn't fill up with poison, he'll maybe be all right."

Maybe! That wasn't good enough, Amos thought. He didn't know how to make Clara understand his feelings when he didn't even understand them himself. All he knew was that he had to do everything he could to keep the boy alive. They were supposed to be enemies, but Amos didn't think of him as an enemy. Except for the nut-brown skin, it could be any boy lying there. It could be Simon.

No, Amos corrected himself; Simon was gone. But the torment Amos had endured as Simon lay dying was something like what he felt now. There was a yearning, an aching need to keep the Indian's life from ebbing away, to grasp that fragile spark and make it stay. Somehow, they had to save the boy.

"It's too late to travel today. Maybe tomorrow . . ." he murmured and turned away from her. He must have dozed off because he jerked when Jonathan nudged him.

"Here's your share," Jonathan said, handing Amos the roasting stick with a sliver of meat on it.

The cooked frog meat, though dry and stringy, left them wanting more, so Amos and Jonathan went hunting again. Amos cut a forked limb from a tree and whittled it to the right shape. The V-shaped prong on the end would pin down a frog long enough for them to catch it.

While Jonathan used the frog gig, Amos fashioned a fish spear and waded into the water. Several fish flashed through the shallows, but he wasn't quick enough to stab any. At last, discouraged, he gave up and went to help Jonathan.

By the time the sun was low in the west, they had caught seven frogs. They returned to camp and soon had the meat spitted over the fire.

As it cooked, Amos walked over and gazed down at the Indian boy. The bandage was stained red and the boy's face had turned as pale as wood ashes. Clara had said he'd probably live, but looking at him, Amos wasn't so sure.

After eating, Amos and Jonathan went to look for another campsite. It had to be far enough inland that the fire wouldn't be seen from the river. They followed the creek until they came to a narrow tributary stream. Amos recalled that last night's Indians had built their fire in a ravine. There were no ravines here, but Amos found a low spot along the stream that would hide the fire's glow.

Sending Jonathan to forage for firewood, Amos went back to camp and used his fire carrier to tote several burning logs to the new site. In only minutes he had a fire blazing. Then he piled up dead leaves for the Indian's bed.

The sun had dropped below the trees by the time he and Jonathan returned to the river. Fog edged out over the Ohio and soon obscured the far shore. Throwing dirt on the remains of the fire, Amos signaled Jonathan to help him pick up the Indian. They set off through the darkening forest with Clara and Queen Anne following. The Indian didn't make a sound, even when they laid him on the bed of leaves.

At the new campsite they relaxed in the fire's comforting light. When Jonathan went to sleep beside Queen Anne, Amos and Clara sat staring into the campfire. Amos thought of his father, as he'd done every day since they'd become separated. Was he still alive? Or were they alone now, left to grow up as best they could without him? If their father was dead, and they were captured by Indians, nobody would ever know what had happened to them.

Amos picked up a twig and tossed it into the live coals where it flared a moment, then crumbled into red ash. He wouldn't give up. He'd believe his father was alive until someone told him otherwise. A smile flickered across his face as he wondered what his father would think about the Indian he'd pulled from the river.

"One of us will have to stay awake and keep the fire going," Amos said after a while.

"You'd better sleep first," Clara said. "I'll wake you later." When Amos nodded agreement, she went on. "Amos, what are we going to do with your Indian?"

"Why do you keep calling him my Indian?"

"Well, if it wasn't for you, he wouldn't be here."

Though Clara's words were meant to scold, they rang in Amos's ears with a wonderful lilt. If it wasn't for him . . . ! Warmth spread through him and he smiled at her across the fire. "We can't do anything with him right now. Let's wait and see if he makes it through the night."

An owl hooted from somewhere far away. Then Clara spoke again. "I've been thinking about Papa all day. Amos, what if he's . . . if he's . . ."

"Dead?" Amos finished in a dull, blunt tone. "There's no use borrowing trouble, Clara. We've got to go on to Marietta. He'll either be there, or the people will have news of the raid."

Amos thought he saw tears in Clara's eyes and it shocked him. She'd always been the strong one, so confident and fearless. In the lonely quiet of the night, their troubles must have overwhelmed her.

"Things will look better in the morning," he said as he stretched out and rested his head on his folded arms. But he wasn't so sure about that. They still wouldn't know about their father. And they'd still be in the wilderness. It was a dangerous place, that was the plain truth, and the Indian boy added to their peril. He had interrupted their journey, could delay it for days; and if he improved, he might do them harm.

Amos expelled a heavy breath. His Uncle Daniel used to say things would either get better or worse by morning. A mocking question went through Amos's mind. How could things get worse?

CHAPTER 8

Amos came awake at Clara's hand on his shoulder. He'd slept soundly, partly because of the previous sleepless night, but even more because the fire's heat and smoke had kept the mosquitoes away. He looked around. The woods were still; not a leaf rustled. Even the night birds had ceased their calling.

Without a word, Clara lay down on a pile of leaves and spread her shawl over her shoulders. Not long after, Amos heard her soft, regular breathing.

He sat up and spread hands to the heat. It wasn't a big fire, but its steady light held back the night shadows. The bed of embers pulsated and glowed like candlelight on red velvet. His thoughts drifted back to their fireplace in Pennsylvania. They had lived their lives around the perpetual fire. They awoke to its crackling warmth, they ate beside it, worked and read and played in its evening light, and went to sleep with its soft gleam flickering on the log walls.

As Amos stared, his father's face seemed to take form in the hot coals. The piercing eyes held a message for Amos; see before you are seen, and remember, there are always Indians.

He rose to his feet and crept around the campfire. The Indian boy lay on his back, his face chiseled sharp against the firelight. Placing a hand on the thin chest, Amos could feel the boy's breaths, though they rattled beneath his fingers. At least he was still alive. They might never find out where or how he was shot, but Amos felt sure he'd been trying to get home. Was there someone worrying and waiting for his return?

When darkness finally paled into day, Amos rose to his feet and stretched. Glancing at the Indian, he stiffened and his breath caught in his throat. The boy's eyes were open and fastened on him. Gleaming like black stone, they held no hint of friendliness or fear.

Amos tried to meet that steadfast gaze with equal calm. He nodded a silent greeting. The Indian continued to stare, and Amos was sure he was trying to piece together where he was and what had happened. Amos edged over and picked up the tin cup of water. He held it out, not knowing whether to help the boy, or wait for him to take the cup himself.

The Indian looked at Amos a moment longer, then turned his head away and closed his eyes.

Placing the cup within the boy's reach, Amos went back to the fire. He watched the Indian, and when several minutes passed without a sign of movement, Amos guessed he was either asleep or too sick to stir. Amos shivered and leaned closer to the fire. He could still see the Indian's eyes, cold and unblinking; the eyes of an enemy.

Amos jumped at a sudden sound. It was only Clara, sitting up, shaking out her rumpled shawl. She scooted closer to the fire and held out her hands to the heat.

"He was awake," Amos said to her, "but he didn't say anything."

"I'd better look at his dressing," Clara said and rose to her feet.

Remembering the Indian's fierce expression, Amos rose and grabbed her arm. "Wait. You'd better not . . . ."

"I'm not afraid of him," Clara said. "After losing all that blood, he's weaker than a newborn colt. When he starts to mend, that's the time to worry."

She went over and knelt beside the boy. As she

lifted the cloth from the wound, the boy tried to push her away. She captured the brown hand and laid it back on his chest.

"You just lie still and don't interfere," she said in the same tone she would have used to tell Jonathan to wash his hands before supper. The boy's jaw tightened, but his hand remained where she had put it.

After replacing the dressing, Clara picked up the cup of water. She slid a hand under the boy's shoulders and pulled him up, then held the cup to his lips. He just stared at her without drinking.

"I don't care whether you drink or not," Clara said to him, just as if he could understand her, "but if you want to get better, you'll have to have liquids."

Their eyes met in silent struggle. At last the boy took a sip of water, then drank until the cup was empty. When Clara lowered him to the ground, his gaze flicked over to Amos. His eyes seemed to be saying something, though Amos had no notion of what it might be.

Clara returned to the fire and stood with her hands on her hips. "Well, it appears that your Indian will live, Amos. Now what do you propose to do with him?" She didn't give Amos time to answer. "He can't walk and he needs food. Where are we going to get food for him? We don't even have any for ourselves. And we should be on our way downriver. The longer we linger in these woods, the more we risk being—"

"Hush, Sister. You'll wake up the Indian," came Jonathan's scolding voice. He stooped to warm himself at the fire. His clothes, as well as his face and arms, were mud-splattered from yesterday's frog hunt. Somehow, though, he'd managed to keep his beaver hat clean.

Amos looked down at his own clothes. He was every bit as dirty. A bath in the creek would be a welcome improvement for both of them.

"What about him, Amos?" Clara asked again.

It was quite a change, her asking Amos for his opinion. Usually she made decisions without consulting anyone. He was slow to answer. "It wouldn't be right to leave him here alone when he's so helpless," he said at last.

"How about leaving him down by the Ohio," Clara suggested. "We could make him a fire, so the Indians would find him."

"What if some of our people find him first?" Amos asked.

"You know very well a boat won't stop on the north bank for anyone."

"Clara, it won't make any difference if we arrive

at Marietta a couple of days later than we planned. Will it?"

Clara frowned at him. "What about food? Every day we spend in the woods, we get hungrier."

Her steady gaze made Amos squirm and he tried to offer some explanation. "I didn't think when I pulled him out of the river . . ." he began.

"You mean, if you had it to do over, you'd let him drown?" Clara asked. Her eyes filled with impatience.

Amos shook his head. There was no question in his mind. He would have saved the Indian, even if he'd had a week to think about it. He couldn't explain how he felt. All he knew was that he couldn't abandon the boy.

Minutes passed, and finally Clara picked up a log and threw it on the fire. It was her signal of surrender. "I'll milk Queen Anne, then we'd better start looking for something to eat. And I'll need some willow bark."

After drinking their fill of milk, Amos and Jonathan headed toward the Ohio. They gathered several strips of willow bark and collected dead wood for their fire. In their wandering search, they came across a black walnut tree. Beneath it were lots of nuts still encased in winter-blackened husks. They used Amos's shirt to carry the precious load back to camp. Scavenging for rocks, they were soon at work cracking open the hulls and the inner shells to get at the rich kernels.

Later, Amos and Jonathan returned to the creek, hoping to capture more frogs. In the backwater they'd hunted the day before, they could see and hear their prey, but overnight the frogs had grown wary. Despite hours of patient stalking, they could capture only four. At Amos's suggestion, they submerged themselves in the gently flowing creek, washing the mud and slime from their bodies and their clothes.

As they lay on the sunny bank and watched the drifting clouds, a flock of Carolina parakeets settled into the nearby trees. The large, green birds fluttered through the foliage, and sometimes, when several landed on the same limb, it cracked beneath their weight.

"If we could catch one of those, we'd have a real supper," Jonathan said.

"You might as well forget about them," Amos said. "We couldn't even get close to them."

"What about Clara's gun? If we had it, we could shoot one from here." Seeing Amos's face, Jonathan hurried on. "I know you couldn't shoot, Amos, but I could. Big as they are, I bet I could hit one, too."

Amos stood up. "When are you going to remember this is Indian country? Shooting off a gun would be like sending them an invitation to come and get us." He grabbed the frog stick and stalked off. It was always there in their midst, he thought, that moment none of them could forget. And everyone made excuses for him. When he saw them shy away from mentioning Simon, saw their careful evasions, he wanted to run away. It wasn't right for them to be burdened by guilt, too. He was to blame, not them.

As they came in sight of camp, Clara ran to meet them. "Amos, he's got a knife. I thought he might want to keep the bullet I took out of him. I was trying to put it in that leather pouch when he pulled a knife out of his boot."

"Did he hurt you, Sister?" Jonathan asked.

"No, I got away from him quick," Clara said. "But I'm not doing another thing for him if he's going to threaten me with a knife."

"I reckon he's feeling better," was all Amos could think to say to her.

"We have to get that knife away from him, Amos," Clara went on. "I'd never be able to sleep, knowing he was lying here, plotting murder. Even that wound doesn't keep him from taking up his savage ways. I told you we should have—"

"Here," Amos broke in, handing her the stick with the cleaned frogs on it. Then he walked toward the Indian. The boy held a short-bladed knife in his right hand, and the look in his eyes reminded Amos of a wounded wildcat. Weak from loss of blood, unable to get away, still he showed no fear.

Amos tried to keep his voice even and firm. "My sister wanted to give you the bullet she took out of your leg. She wasn't snooping. You'd better give me the knife."

"He can't understand you, Amos," Clara called from a safe distance.

"He may not understand the words," Amos replied, "but he knows what I want." He took a step closer, then stooped down and rested his arms on his knees. He held out his hand, showing his open, empty palm.

The boy's eyes flitted to Amos's hand, then back to his face, and a low, growling sound broke the silence. The words were unintelligible, but there was no denying the scorn in the Indian's voice.

Amos felt a flicker of admiration. The boy must be in terrible pain, yet still he found the strength to challenge them. It would be too dangerous to try to take the knife away, Amos knew. His only hope was to coax the boy into giving it up.

Before Amos could speak, the Indian let out a soft, shuddering breath. His hostility seemed to melt like butter in a hot skillet. Though he made no other sound, his eyes narrowed and the hand holding the knife fluttered upward in feeble protest.

Amos could almost feel the power of the pain. He looked around at Clara. "Haven't you got something in your bag to help him?"

"No, the medicine box was on the boat," she said. "All I can do is change the compress. But I'm not doing anything until he gives up that knife."

Amos agreed with Clara that none of them should go near the boy as long as he wielded the weapon. To the Indian, they were the enemy. Amos extended his hand again. "Let me have the knife."

A grim defiance darkened the boy's face once again. He stared at Amos without moving.

He doesn't understand the words, Amos thought, but he gets the meaning. He's thinking over his situation and trying to decide what to do. The moment of decision came sooner than Amos expected.

In slow, clumsy movements, the boy laid the knife on his chest, turned it around, and picked it up by the blade. Then he reached out and laid the knife in Amos's waiting hand.

As Amos's fingers closed over the warm handle,

he let out a quiet sigh. But the feeling of triumph died when he saw the Indian's face.

Despite the look of outward calm, the boy appeared to shrink back within himself. He was beaten. He had shown weakness. In some strange way, Amos understood. The boy had willingly given up his weapon to the enemy, and it shamed him.

Amos hefted the knife. With its wide blade and thick bone handle, it was a knife made for killing. His gaze slid from the weapon to the Indian. Then he made a surprising decision of his own. He grasped the knife by its blade and held it out to the Indian boy. Behind him, he heard Clara gasp.

The Indian's eyes widened, then he expelled a slow breath and took the offered knife. He raised up high enough to slide it into his moccasin before he sagged to the ground again and closed his eyes.

"Why in heaven's thunder did you give it back to him?" Clara blurted out.

"He's not going to hurt anyone," Amos said. "Come on over here. You'd better see about this bandage."

CHAPTER 9

Clara continued to complain about the Indian and his weapon, but Amos pretended not to hear. He and Jonathan cracked the remaining walnuts and picked out the kernels while the frog meat cooked. After accepting only a few nuts and a cup of water, the Indian sank into a deep sleep.

While Clara went to the creek to bathe, Amos and Jonathan scoured the woods around the campsite for firewood. Twilight had come by the time they'd gathered enough fuel to last the night. They cleared a place by the fire for a game of marbles and became so engrossed in their play that they didn't notice Clara had returned until she spoke.

"Someone's mighty interested in your marbles," she said to them. When they looked up, she waved a thumb over her shoulder at the Indian. The boy had risen up on one elbow to watch them, but as soon as they looked in his direction, he turned away.

"He's probably never seen any marbles before," Amos said.

"He has a blue stone in that pouch he wears around his neck," Clara said. "It's as smooth as a marble, but flat."

"It must be important to him," Amos said. "Especially since he pulled a knife on you for looking at it." He grinned at her, then went on. "I wonder what tribe he belongs to."

"What difference does it make," Clara said. "The important thing to know is that he's a savage."

Amos didn't contradict Clara, even though he disagreed with her. The Indian was just a boy like him, but injured and alone, and, he thought, a little afraid. He gathered up his marbles and dropped them into the pouch.

"Did you notice his moccasins?" Jonathan remarked. "How do you reckon he colored the deerskin red?"

"Blackberries will dye anything red," Clara told him. "Even wood."

"You'd make a real good Indian," Amos said with a solemn face.

"I have no aspirations to be a savage," Clara said and turned her attention to her knapsack. Piece by piece, she emptied the contents out on the ground. When she pulled out the pistol, she cast a sideways glance at Amos. "I wonder if this would . . . surely the powder's dry by this time."

She tilted the barrel downward over a corner of her shawl, tapping it gently until the lead ball and cloth patch fell out. When the lump of powder followed, she picked it up and crumbled it between her fingers. "It's ruined," she said.

Amos's stomach tightened and he jammed his hands into his pockets. He hated the sight of the pistol and, without powder, it was useless anyway. Maybe she would leave it there in the woods when they continued their journey.

Clara blew into the priming hole, then released a loud breath. "Amos, I'm as dense as a lop-eared mule."

"What are you talking about?"

"I forgot about . . . right here on the gun hammer is a flint. We could've made a fire anytime." As if to prove her words, she squeezed the trigger and the flint struck steel, throwing off a bright spark.

Amos flinched and his heart started thumping in his chest. He should've taken the thing from her on the boat and thrown it overboard. She'd keep it for sure now. He rose to his feet and stalked off into the deepening darkness.

Not thinking of where he was headed, Amos soon found himself on the bank of the Ohio. Moonlight through the trees cast dense, black shadows on the river. Back in Pennsylvania, it would have been a perfect night to play hide-and-seek in the haymow, or sit in a tree and listen to the whippoorwills talk. He sagged down on the riverbank, remembering Simon. If only he could live last year over again. There would be no haunting memories, no awful guilt. He sat there a long time, thinking how Simon would have loved the moonlight and the rippling river.

After a while, he got up and tramped along the riverbank, his thoughts wandering like the night wind through the trees. A noise overhead made him freeze in his tracks. Looking up, he saw dark shapes silhouetted against the glowing sky. It was a flock of Carolina parakeets roosting in a massive sycamore.

Maybe they were like chickens, Amos thought, listless and half-blind in the dark. If he was stealthy and patient, he might be able to catch one. He crept over to the sycamore tree, then pulled himself up onto a low limb. Two birds squatted on a bough just a couple of feet above him, their heads tucked into their wing feathers.

Moving as slowly and quietly as a snail, Amos

inched his back up along the rough tree trunk until he stood upright. Then, grasping a branch with one hand, he reached out and snatched the nearest parakeet by the neck. The bird began to flap its powerful wings, pulling Amos off balance, and he lost his grip on the branch. His feet slipped out from under him and he fell, crashing through the leafy branches on his way to the ground.

Though the thick layer of dead leaves cushioned his landing, for a moment he was too dazed to know what had happened. Then he grinned. He was still clutching the parakeet. Overhead, the frightened birds floundered through the foliage, breaking off leaves and small limbs, squawking their alarm. He hoped there were no Indians near enough to hear all that commotion. The bird in his hand made no sound at all. Eager to show everyone his catch, he sprang to his feet and cut back toward camp.

The fire had died down to a few smoldering logs and Clara sat before it, staring into the embers. Jonathan and the Indian were sleeping. At the sound of Amos's bare feet rustling through the dry leaves, Clara jerked upright.

"What's that in your hand?" she asked.

"It's a Carolina parakeet. It must weigh five or six pounds."

"How in the world . . ." Clara exclaimed.

Amos grinned at her. "They'd already gone to roost. I just grabbed one and held on. It managed to knock me out of a tree, but it didn't get away." He took the dead bird and lodged it in the crotch of a nearby tree, then came back to the fire. As he sat down, Clara spoke again.

"Don't you think we should be getting on to Marietta, Amos? We've been here two days and there's no telling how much ground we have to cover yet."

"How is the Indian?" Amos asked, rather than try to answer her question.

"I gave him some willow bark tea. He just sits and stares at me. It's scary. There's no way of knowing what he's thinking behind those wild eyes."

"He's probably wondering what we're doing here in the woods, the same as we're wondering about him."

"Amos, you don't mean for us to take him along, do you?"

Amos wasn't used to making decisions, but if he left it up to Clara, she'd want to leave the Indian. In Amos's mind, abandoning the boy would be almost as bad as leaving Jonathan behind. "We can take him with us until he can get along on his own. I expect he'll be able to walk with some help."

"The more he heals, the more dangerous he'll be," Clara warned him. "He's still got that knife, and he hates us for sure. It wouldn't—"

"Did you ever think that maybe he's afraid of us?"

"Afraid! Why, he wouldn't have the sense to be afraid of a she-bear with three cubs."

"He probably doesn't trust us either," Amos went on, ignoring her remark. "If only we could talk to him, make him understand what we intend to do."

"Sassafras, Amos! You can't reason with a savage."

Amos slapped at a mosquito. He just couldn't think of the Indian as Clara did. Even though the boy was different from them, somehow it didn't seem very important here in the woods. The only thing that mattered was surviving. Amos recalled their meager supper, wondering how long the Indian had gone without food. At first light, he'd clean the bird and get it roasting. The plump fowl would go a long way toward easing everyone's hunger.

"Well, if we're not going to decide anything, you might as well go to sleep," Clara said, turning her back on him.

It was still pitch-dark when Clara shook him awake. "Everything's quiet," she said, then curled up in the leaves.

Amos rose and walked around the fire, pausing to look at the Indian, then Jonathan and Queen

Anne. The Jersey gazed up at him, her eyes reflecting the fire's glow. How lucky they were, he thought, that they had the cow. She not only gave them milk, but she was a constant reminder of the family life they used to have. Amos added a log to the fire, then sat down to wait for daybreak.

As soon as the woods began to brighten, Amos took the bird to the nearby stream and set to work. He laid aside some orange and yellow head feathers and several long, green tailfeathers for Clara. She didn't have any use for them here in the woods, but she could carry them on to Marietta. They were pretty enough to use for decoration, or they could be fashioned into quill pens.

Juices from the roasting fowl were dripping into the fire by the time the others began to stir. When Clara was wide awake, Amos handed her the feathers.

"Aren't they nice," she said, and took a yellow one and stuck it in her hair. Then she noticed the Indian staring at her. "What's he looking at!" she said, her hands settling on her hips.

Amos couldn't pass up the chance to tease her. "I'll bet he's thinking you're as pretty as an Indian girl, with that feather in your hair."

Clara dismissed his words with a wave of her hand and walked away toward the stream.

While Amos was turning the bird on its spit, he heard a noise and looked around. The Indian had managed to sit up. Then he turned over on his hands and knees and pushed himself to his feet. Swaying from side to side, he remained on his feet, Amos was sure, through sheer willpower alone.

Amos stepped toward him and held out his hand, offering to help. Reading a warning in the boy's eyes, he dropped his hand away. In spite of the silent rebuke, he felt a tingle of satisfaction. He and the Indian might not be able to talk back and forth, but they'd certainly understood each other just now. From the corner of his eye, Amos watched the boy take a few faltering steps, then turn his back on the campsite and massage the injured leg.

The brief exchange set Amos to wondering as he returned to the fire. Maybe if they kept talking, they'd eventually understand each other. There had to be a way for them to communicate.

Jonathan sat up and plopped the beaver hat on his head. "I see Red Moccasin is up and walking."

"What did you call him?"

"Red Moccasin . . . on account of his shoes. Even an Indian has to have a name."

He's right, Amos thought. They ought to call him something besides just "the Indian." The name

Red Moccasin would do until they learned his Indian name.

Later, when Amos pronounced the roasted bird ready to eat, they gathered around the fire for the best meal they'd had since they left Wheeling town. Amos broke off a browned chunk of the bird and went toward the Indian.

The injured boy had returned to his bed of leaves and lay with his eyes closed, but they came open at Amos's approach. His gaze never left Amos's face, even as he accepted the cooked meat.

"This ought to make you feel better," Amos said.

The boy uttered a harsh grunt that might have been a word, then bit into the meat.

After the bird's skeleton had been picked clean and the bones chewed to splinters, Clara spoke again about them continuing downriver.

"I think we should stay here one more day," Amos said.

"We need to get to Marietta," Clara said, "and find out about—"

"No need to be in a hurry," Amos broke in, then stopped. He'd started to say there was no need to hurry to Marietta just to get bad news. Until they got there, they could believe their father was alive. "Right now we need food worse than we need to get to Marietta," he finished.

"I could catch some more frogs," Jonathan said.

"And I might be able to catch another parakeet," Amos added. He'd already made up his mind to go out at sundown and locate their roosting place.

Looking from one to the other, Clara grumbled under her breath, reluctantly giving in. "All right. One more day, but then I'm going to Marietta, with or without you."

The Indian must have used up all his strength because he lay on his bed, hardly moving. He appeared to be sleeping when Clara and Jonathan went off to collect wood.

Amos walked down to the bank of the Ohio in hopes of seeing or hearing the parakeets. From the edge of the forest shade, he squinted at the noonday sun sparkling on the water. The Ohio was wide here and steep, wooded banks lined the far shore. It was as peaceful as a pasturefield at dusk.

He proceeded upstream, watching and listening for the parakeets. Not finding any, he climbed onto the limb of a willow tree leaning over the water, where he could view the whole river without exposing himself. What he saw almost made him fall into the water. A flatboat was skimming downstream at a good speed, hugging the south shore.

As it came closer, Amos could make out figures

on the deck. There were no women or children in sight, only men staring and pointing across the river at the north bank. Some knelt at the railing, aiming their long-barreled rifles in that direction.

Leaning out as far as he dared, Amos gazed along the bank on his side of the river. A movement caught his eye and he sucked in a noisy breath. A mile or so away on a flat, treeless bluff, three Indians were standing in the bright sun, watching the flatboat.

Amos's gaze swung back to the boat. It was opposite him now and he looked with longing at the men who could save him. But he knew they'd never stop. The Indians were too close. Besides, he couldn't leave without Clara and Jonathan.

He watched the boat pass, then focused once more on the Indians. A moment longer they stared at the river, then abruptly turned their backs on it. Amos strained to see if they were coming downstream, but they had disappeared in the trees. His throat felt as dry as scorched leather. Even if he hid from them, they were bound to smell the smoke from the campfire. He had to get back and warn the others. Jumping from the tree to shore, he scrambled into the woods and sped toward camp.

CHAPTER 10

The telltale odor of smoke burned Amos's nostrils long before he reached camp. Grabbing a stick, he dashed straight to the fire and scattered the blazing logs. Then he fell on his knees and smothered the flames with dirt and damp leaves.

Only then did he look around for the others. Clara and Jonathan were gone, along with the cow, but the Indian lay on his bed, watching Amos.

"Where are they?" Amos demanded.

The boy stared at him a moment, then extended his right arm, palm down, fingers outstretched. In a slight, upward movement, he gestured off through the woods.

Amos turned and trotted off in that direction. He hadn't gone far when he heard them coming. Clara was leading the cow and talking, and Jonathan followed with his arms full of wood.

When Clara saw Amos, she stopped. "What's wrong?"

"We've got to get away from here," Amos said, beckoning them forward. "There's Indians on this side of the river and they may be coming our way."

Jonathan ran up beside Amos. "What'll they do to us, Amos?"

"They're not going to catch us," Amos said, and knocked the wood out of Jonathan's arms. "Forget that. I put out the fire."

Back in camp, Amos went to the Indian and motioned him to get up. "Come on. We're leaving."

Hiding his pain, the boy labored to his feet. He rested his weight on his uninjured leg and waited.

"Why don't we leave him here?" Clara said.

Amos had considered it. After all, the boy hadn't shown any signs of gratitude for what they'd done for him, pulling him from the river, doctoring him. But they had to take him along for their own safety. He looked on them as the enemy, and he'd certainly tell the other Indians about them.

"No, he has to go with us," Amos told her.

When he stepped over to the Indian, the boy understood what he must do. He raised his arm and laid it across Amos's shoulders. With Amos's arm around the boy's waist, the two of them set off through the trees.

The Indian hobbled beside Amos in silence, pausing once to pick up a stick to use for a cane. It helped him balance his weight and made their walking a little easier. His only acknowledgment of pain was an occasional soft grunt.

A little later, Amos noticed blood trickling down the Indian's leg and he stopped. The Indian sagged to the ground, his face pale, his breathing uneven.

"We'll rest here," Amos told Clara. "You'd better look at his wound."

While Clara tightened the bandage, the Indian lay with closed eyes, his face taut and gray. Clara looked at Amos. "How do you know the Indians are coming this way? Maybe they went upstream. We could hide here and wait until—"

"We can't let them catch up," Amos said. He knew they were leaving a trail that anyone could follow, but there was no way of avoiding it. Their only hope was to keep moving, to stay ahead of the Indians.

Clara stood with her hands on her hips, watching the Indian. "He hates us, Amos. He's forgotten he'd be at the bottom of the river if it wasn't for you."

Amos gazed at the Indian, seeing only a boy like himself. "I'll bet we could be friends . . . ."

"You'd better start thinking of him as your enemy, Amos. Why, you couldn't trust him to . . ."

Amos stopped listening when he saw the Indian's face. For a moment, the glittering eyes mirrored Clara's own hostility and distrust; then, like the closing of a door, a mask of indifference settled down to hide the boy's thoughts.

They continued to follow the westering river. It was well after sunset before they stopped in a stand of willows that almost obscured the Ohio. Leafy branches trailed on the ground, closing in a grassy, secluded space. They decided to spend the night there.

"I'm hungry," Jonathan said, sprawling on the ground.

"I've got a few walnuts left," Clara said, opening her knapsack. "Gather some tinder and I'll start a fire."

"No!" Amos almost shouted. "We can't take the chance."

"But Amos, we're a long way from the other camp," Clara said.

"Not so far that we can't be found," he replied. He pointed to the injured boy. "Those Indians are probably looking for him. Smoke would lead them straight to us."

No use mentioning that if the Indians had turned downstream, they'd probably smelled the smoke and already found the other campsite. They might be on the trampled trail this very minute. One thought gave Amos hope. The Indians couldn't track them in the dark.

Lack of food worried Amos as much as the Indians did. Though Queen Anne's milk relieved their hunger pangs for a while, it didn't satisfy the deep craving for solid food. They were getting weaker every day. The few nuts they had left were divided up, giving each of them only a bite.

Night passed in aching discomfort. Only the cow appeared rested and ready to continue at dawn. Although the Indian seemed to move with less pain, he accepted Amos's help once they started walking.

The sun rode high in a blue sky when they came upon a shimmering meadow. A fleeting flash of brown told them they'd flushed a grazing deer. Wildflowers glowed among the tall grasses and as they stepped into the open, a flock of passenger pigeons lifted into the air. What a beautiful spot, Amos thought, turning his face up to the sun's warmth.

Like persons on a summer outing, they roamed over the bright meadow, forgetting for a few moments their hunger and their fear. The Indian let go of Amos and hobbled along with his stick cane. When Clara dropped Queen Anne's rope, she began to browse on the rich grass.

Wandering across the sunlit space, they came together under an oak tree at the meadow's western edge. The Indian, last to arrive, came carrying a lumpy, white root in his hand. Bits of dirt still clung to it. He walked over and held it out to Amos, then pointed a finger at his open mouth.

Amos accepted the offered food and was about to bite into it when Clara rushed over and grabbed his hand.

"Don't, Amos. It could be poisonous."

The Indian stood motionless, seeming to ponder Clara's words and actions. Then he seized the root from Amos's hand, and with his eyes never wavering from Clara's face, he took a big bite and chewed it up. He hobbled a few feet away and sat down, and, while Clara stood there glaring at him, continued to eat until the root was gone.

Amos regretted Clara's open lack of trust, but he was elated, too. The boy did understand them, maybe not the words, but the meaning behind the words. He'd comprehended Clara's warning and responded with a clear, pointed answer of his own. And it was just as Amos suspected. The boy did know where to find food. They had to try to communicate with him. They could learn from him.

Amos walked over and knelt by the boy. He laid a hand on his own chest and said, "My name is

Amos . . . Amos." He turned and motioned to Jonathan who stood behind him. "This is Jonathan," he said to the Indian. Then he pointed to Clara. "Her name is Clara."

"He doesn't understand you, Amos," Jonathan said.

Amos ignored his brother and again touched his chest. "I'm Amos."

The Indian frowned and looked from Amos to Jonathan. Then he laid his hand against his bare chest and spoke several words that sounded to Amos like a saw biting into wood.

Amos grinned. "I can't pronounce it but it must be your name. And I'm Amos. Pleased to meet you."

"Let's just call him Red Moccasin," Jonathan said.

"I guess we'll have to," Amos replied. He turned back to the Indian and pointed to the knee-high moccasins. "My brother has named you Red Moccasin." He leaned forward and lightly tapped the boy's chest. "Red Moccasin."

After a moment, the Indian shook his head and repeated the unpronounceable name. Amos grinned at him. They weren't exactly talking, but they were understanding each other.

"I wonder if he could find some more of that

root," Jonathan said. "I'm hungry enough to eat anything, even Indian food."

Amos pointed to his open mouth and said, "Is there any more of that root around here?" He waved an arm toward the meadow.

The boy studied Amos with cold eyes, then got to his feet and limped off. They watched him work his way around the meadow, pushing the weeds aside with his cane, sometimes disappearing when he knelt on the ground. He returned with several roots and dropped them on the ground in front of Amos. Without looking at any of them, he walked away.

Picking up one of the roots, Amos brushed off the clinging dirt and took a bite. It tasted like sawdust, but at least it took away the empty feeling in his stomach. Jonathan grabbed one of the roots, then pulled himself up onto a low tree limb and sat gazing out over the meadow as he ate. Clara, still skeptical, nibbled hers as if she expected any minute to fall down dead. The warm sun drained away their energy and purpose, and for a few minutes, they forgot the Indians that might be pursuing them.

Amos was the first to remember. "We'd better move on," he said, rising to his feet. "The Indians—"

Jonathan interrupted him from his perch on the limb above them. "I don't see any Indians except Red Moccasin."

"You won't see them if they don't want to be seen," Amos said. "Come on down. We can't waste any more time here. Besides, see those clouds." He pointed at the sky. "There's rain coming."

As they walked, the dim light in the forest turned to semi-darkness. Wind whistled overhead and the rain worked its way through the canopy of leaves and drenched them. It was a cold rain, as if it had blown across a snowfield. They shivered and pulled their scant clothes tighter around them, trying to hold on to their bodies' warmth.

The Indian had refused Amos's offer of help. He hobbled along behind the cow, head down, bare shoulders hunched against the rain. Although he gave no sign of it, Amos knew he, too, was suffering from the cold.

Wet, chill leaves on the forest floor set Amos's bare feet tingling. He wished they could stop and make a fire, but the thought of Indians somewhere behind them kept him moving. If the storm intensified, though, they'd have to find shelter. When Amos looked toward the Ohio, it was shrouded in mist. Maybe this weather was a blessing, he told himself. The storm would surely obscure their trail, and in the worst of it, the pursuing Indians would have to seek shelter, too.

At last, weary and shivering, Amos stopped and

waited for the others. "I think we'd better let the storm pass on. We wouldn't want to lose sight of the river."

"Maybe we can find a tree that'll keep off some of the rain," Clara said. She was shivering so hard that her teeth clattered together. Jonathan, rainwater dripping from his hat, moved over beside her. She reached out and hugged him against her.

"You're warm, Sister," he said, snuggling closer.

"Do you think we could start a fire?" Clara asked, seeming to want Amos to decide things now.

"We can't risk it," Amos said. "The rain would probably put it out anyway."

They took refuge under an elm tree, pulling Queen Anne in among them as they huddled together for warmth. Red Moccasin remained apart, rubbing his injured leg and studying the misty woods.

Early darkness and stinging cold descended upon them. Jonathan curled himself against Queen Anne's belly and pushed his bare feet into the warm hollow between her udder and her leg. Amos, feet resting on the cow's neck, felt her moving, and from time to time, heard her teeth grinding her cud. They endured the night in silence, too weak to complain.

The only sign of day breaking was a slight graying of the forest gloom. Rain still fell, a steady drizzle that felt like a cold knife slicing through to their bones. Amos saw Clara rise to her feet and grab hold of the Jersey to steady herself. Her face was flushed and her eyes glittered like glass.

"Are you all right?" he asked.

"Yes, I'm just tired," she said without looking at him. She laid an arm around Queen Anne's neck and closed her eyes.

They set off in a straggling line through the trees, Amos leading, casting quick glances over his shoulder to make sure they were staying together. He worried that it was only a matter of time until the Indians caught up with them. They had to get to Marietta before that happened.

Once, when Amos paused to look back, he saw Red Moccasin stop and stare off through the trees. Did he see something, hear something the rest of them couldn't detect? Their eyes met for a moment, and it seemed to Amos the Indian was saying, "Not yet, but soon." Amos walked on, his hope seeping away like water through sand.

They traveled for some time before Amos turned again to look down their back trail. There was no movement, no sign of trouble. But suddenly Clara, who had been walking beside the cow, sagged across Queen Anne's back, then slid off and fell to the ground.

Amos rushed over to her. "Clara, what's wrong? Clara . . . can you hear me?" He shook her until her eyes opened.

She wet her lips with her tongue before speaking. "I feel so bad, Amos. I don't think I can walk any more."

Amos laid a hand on her cheek, then jerked it away. She was as hot as a boiling teakettle. He slid an arm under her shoulders and tried to raise her up, but she mumbled something and shook her head.

"What's wrong with her, Amos?" Jonathan asked. His wide eyes bored into Amos. "Clara never gets sick."

"She's got a fever," Amos said. He stared down at her. Clara had always been the strong one in the family, reliable and solid as stone. Amos knew these past grueling days without enough food had weakened her, but he hadn't noticed until now that she was as scrawny as a scarecrow. No wonder she was sick. He marveled that she'd been able to come this far. Now more than ever, they needed to find shelter.

As he gathered her up in his arms, her hot cheek fell against his shoulder. She was afire with fever. He wouldn't tell Jonathan, but he was afraid for her. Maybe he was even more afraid for himself. Losing her would be like losing Simon, only worse.

Amos signaled Jonathan to bring Clara's knapsack and the cow, then walked on with his light, limp burden. The Indian would just have to get along the best he could, and if he decided to walk off, Amos wouldn't be able to stop him.

At last, numb with cold and fatigue, Amos stopped. They had to get out of this rain. Up ahead, he spied a beech tree, its horizontal limbs thick with foliage. It would provide some shelter. Amos strode on and lowered Clara down next to the tree's smooth, gray trunk, pulling her shawl closer around her. Jonathan came up with Queen Anne, while the Indian hobbled along behind.

"Why'd you stop, Amos? Is Clara . . ." Jonathan's voice cracked and tears welled in his eyes.

"No, she's just the same," Amos told him. "But I thought this tree would keep off the rain. We'll wait a while and see if it stops."

Amos's mind whirled, imagining the narrowing gap between them and the Indians. The endless walking, the days and nights of hunger and rain and mosquitoes and cold had all come down to this, a frantic race for freedom. For a moment, Amos had the sinking feeling that none of them would ever reach Marietta. Then he thought of his father. They had to get to Marietta and find out if he was still alive.

CHAPTER 11

$\approx\approx\approx\approx\approx\approx\approx\approx\approx\approx\approx\approx\approx$

Dusk settled over them, with rain falling soft and steady. Clara's weak voice occasionally broke the quiet, and once when Amos leaned over to feel her cheek, she flailed out and struck him hard on the nose.

"Melinda, don't you dare tell or I'll . . ."

"She's out of her head, Amos," Jonathan whispered.

"It's the fever," Amos said. The wandering phrases, the glazed, unseeing eyes indicated she was getting worse, not better. He was afraid that without rest and nourishing food, her body could not fight off the illness. Just when they needed to travel swiftly, she couldn't travel at all. She was too sick to sit up, let alone walk. Amos considered the idea of going on alone to Marietta and bringing back help, but he knew he couldn't leave Clara and

Jonathan there with hostile Indians on their trail. Besides, he didn't know what Red Moccasin might do.

Amos watched the boy rubbing his injured leg, calm, remote, accepting the pain without complaint. He's used to this hard land, Amos thought. When he's hurting, when bad weather batters him, when there's no food, he simply waits for better times. And why not? Amos reasoned. There wasn't anything else to do except wait. A heavy weariness crept over Amos and he lay flat on the ground and closed his eyes. He'd wait too. Things would be better by morning . . . or worse.

When Amos woke, his first thought was of Clara. She lay as still as a baby rabbit. A hand to her cheek told him the fever still raged. He had to do something. But what? Clara was the doctor. He wished he'd paid more attention to her doctoring and her herbs. Then he remembered she'd made Red Moccasin a tea from willow bark. He'd gotten better, so maybe willow tea would help her too. But it would mean starting a fire. They could burn it just long enough to heat the water, then put it out right afterward. It'd be risky, but they had to do something. He went to Jonathan and shook him awake.

"How is she?" were Jonathan's first words.

"She's still got fever," Amos said. "We're going to make a fire and boil some willow bark."

Jonathan looked around. "What about the Indians?"

"We have to fix her some medicine," Amos said. "Turn over one of those dead logs and see if there's some dry wood on the underside. I'll go get the willow bark."

Amos hurried down to the bank of the Ohio, eyes and ears alert to the woods around him. By the time he returned with a cup of water and several strips of willow bark, Jonathan had already collected a good-sized pile of tinder.

A sudden thought hit Amos like a thunderbolt and his eyes slid over to Clara's knapsack. Not until this moment had he considered that he'd have to pick up the pistol and pull the trigger in order to start the fire. He tried to reason away his rising fear. It wasn't the same gun, he told himself, but the thought was no consolation. The other pistol had disappeared after the accident, and nobody had mentioned it again. But Amos hadn't forgotten it. Even now, a painful image arose in his mind of the empty wooden pegs over the fireplace. After the accident, those pegs had been a daily reminder of the gun that wasn't there.

Hurrying, so that he wouldn't have time to think

about it, Amos went and reached into the knapsack. The touch of cold metal sent a shiver through him and when he pulled out the weapon, it slipped from his fingers. He left it where it fell and backed away. He couldn't do it, even to help Clara. Ignoring his brother and the watching Indian, he knelt beside Clara and laid his hand on her hot forehead. He wished he could apologize to her.

A few minutes later he heard the sound of flint striking steel, and without looking, knew that Jonathan was doing what he'd been unable to do. When the clacking sounds finally stopped, Amos turned to watch.

Jonathan was on his knees, head almost touching the ground, blowing on the sparking tinder. A thin, blue spiral of smoke rose and wafted away on the morning air. Then the flame grew until the whole tinder pile was ablaze. It was a good thing for Clara that Jonathan wasn't afraid of guns.

While Jonathan fed twigs into the fire, Amos shaved a handful of willow bark and dropped it into the cup of water. As soon as the liquid came to a boil, he lifted it out of the flames and covered it with a stone. Then he helped Jonathan smother the fire with wet leaves.

Waiting for the willow tea to steep, Amos watched the surrounding forest. It hardly seemed

126

possible that Indians could be stalking them, the woods were so serene. But he knew they were in greater peril than at any time since they'd come into the Ohio country. Unable to travel because of Clara, they were like beaver in a trap. Red Moccasin must have guessed they were running from Indians because he watched and listened too, as if waiting for something, or someone.

Time was their other enemy. Each day without food left them weaker than the day before. Amos felt shaky from the steady drain of going without food. He thought the hunger must be affecting his brain too, because sometimes his thoughts seemed to wander through past and present and future, unguided, beyond his control.

When the willow tea had cooled down, Amos took a stick and scraped out most of the bark. Then he lifted Clara's head and held the cup to her lips. She resisted at first, but he coaxed and commanded her until she had finished it. Even if the willow bark didn't help the fever, he thought, the warm liquid would soothe her empty stomach.

Amos milked Queen Anne and gave Clara a few sips, then he and Jonathan drank their fill. When Red Moccasin refused the offered cup, Amos squirted the rest of the cow's milk out on the ground.

Clara needed rest, and Amos knew they had to find a hiding place to wait out her illness. The river had been their guide, their sanctuary in the unknown wilderness, but now it harbored the enemy. Their only choice was to leave it. He told Jonathan what he intended to do, then picked up Clara and headed away from the Ohio. He was relieved to see Red Moccasin fall in behind Jonathan and the cow.

The straggling party walked until they came across a stream gurgling between great, rounded sandstone boulders. A narrow strip of sunlight slanted through the foliage and warmed the ground. Amos laid Clara down. There was shelter here, and cover from searching eyes. If they could hide their tracks, maybe the Indians would pass them by.

Leaving Jonathan to dredge out a pool for drinking, Amos headed down their backtrail, pausing along the way to break a leafy branch from a tree. At the spot where they'd spent the night, he began sweeping away their telltale tracks. Maybe the Indians he'd seen hadn't even come downstream, but he had to try to cover their trail just to be sure. Even if it didn't fool them, it might delay them for a while.

He erased the signs of their passing as best he

could, all the way back to the stone shelter. When he saw Jonathan kneeling beside Clara, crooning soft words to her like a mother soothing a sleepy child, tears welled in his eyes. She appeared to be worse than before. Chills racked her body and her cheeks were red with heat. Filling the cup at the stream, Amos dribbled the cool water between her dry lips. It seemed to quiet her.

As he sat down, Amos heard the marble sack rattling against his leg. He pulled open the drawstring and emptied the marbles into his hand. They felt smooth and cool, like polished metal. He picked out the green agate shooter and rolled it between his thumb and fingers, while his fist closed around the other marbles.

He realized Red Moccasin was studying him from across the stream. The boy glanced from Amos's face to the fistful of marbles, then back to Amos's face again. There was veiled puzzlement in the black eyes. Amos thought how strange it was that he and the boy understood each other without speaking the same language. Tone of voice, eyes, hands conveyed their thoughts almost as well as words. Just now, Red Moccasin is wondering about the marbles, Amos thought. But even if we could communicate in words, I could never make him understand about Simon.

The marbles had gathered warmth in Amos's hand and for a brief moment their silky-smooth heat comforted him. Then he channeled them back into the pouch and pulled the drawstring. His knife and his marbles were the only things he had left of his former life. No, he thought, he had Jonathan and Clara, and the cow. And when they reached Marietta, he'd have his father once again.

Amos came alert when he saw Red Moccasin lift his head, his whole body poised, listening. Amos listened too, eyes darting here and there. The woods seemed eerily quiet.

Suddenly, and almost silently, they were surrounded. Indians, wearing only deerskin leggings and moccasins and carrying rifles, closed in from all sides.

Amos rose to his feet, clamping his jaws shut to keep his teeth from chattering. Out of the corner of his eye, he saw Jonathan edging toward him. Without taking his eyes off the Indians, he reached out and gave his brother a push. "Stay with Clara," he murmured. Then he squared his shoulders and took a step forward, setting his mind to face whatever would come.

The Indians seemed to take Amos's stance as a challenge. They moved closer, tightening the circle around him alone. One man, no taller than Amos but much heavier and with bulging muscles, shoved Amos backwards. Immediately, rough hands propelled him forward again.

Amos would have fallen if an Indian hadn't caught him in his arms. For a moment, Amos stared up into the dark, laughing eyes, and he smelled the man's closeness, a mixed odor of sweat and grease and wood smoke. Then he was sent spinning across the circle again. The men laughed out loud at his awkward attempts to stay on his feet.

When Amos bumped against one of the men, he put out his hands and pushed hard. The man stumbled backwards, grinning. They seemed to think it was a game, but Amos felt helpless and frustrated and angry. He glared at them and balled his hands into fists.

Just then, someone snatched Amos's knife from its sheath. Spinning around, Amos saw a man rubbing his thumb across the shiny blade. He grinned at Amos as he slipped the knife into his high-topped moccasin. A moment later, someone seized the marble pouch from Amos's belt. The thief, a lean-faced man wearing a necklace of small, white shells, loosened the drawstring and dumped the marbles into his hand. He rattled them together and laughed at the pleasant sound.

A sharp voice from beyond the circle halted the men's rough game. They grinned at Amos but there was no more jostling. Amos stood still, breathing hard, as a man with a wrinkled face as dark as the forest soil came into view. His shoulder-length hair was streaked with gray. Colored beads decorated his deerskin shirt, and fringe on the sides of his leggings danced at every step.

The man's sweeping gaze took in Amos and Jonathan and Clara. Then his eyes, bright with an inner fire, came to rest on Red Moccasin.

As the man and boy conversed in their harsh-sounding language, Amos stood on quivering legs, his stomach churning until he thought he might be sick. The anger he'd felt toward the men melted away into fear. He and Clara and Jonathan were prisoners, there was no doubt about that, and all the walking and hiding and striving had been for nothing. They were in the hands of the Indians, with no hope of escape—or rescue. With a longing that was pure pain, he felt sure he would never see his father again.

CHAPTER 12

While Red Moccasin and the old man talked, Amos watched, observing the harmony between them. They seemed to know each other very well. Red Moccasin's face softened once and smoothed into what could almost have been a smile. Now more than ever, Amos wished he could understand their language. Was Red Moccasin telling the old man about being pulled from the river? Maybe when the Indians learned about him saving Red Moccasin's life, they'd let the three of them go.

Amos edged over and dropped down beside Jonathan. He was relieved to see that Clara was still sleeping. Nothing was as important as her getting well. He swung his gaze to the Indians, fearing what they might do, but the men simply ignored their prisoners. One started a fire while two others tied a deer's carcass on a tree branch, then set to work gutting and cleaning the animal.

"What are they going to do with us, Amos?"

"I don't know, but I think they'll probably take us back to their village."

"Will they hurt us?" Jonathan's voice was only a whisper, and he was shaking so hard that Amos laid an arm around his shoulders.

"Don't go borrowing trouble," Amos told him. "They had a chance to hurt me, but they didn't." He remembered his father saying that Indians took white children to replace children they'd lost, but now wasn't the time to tell Jonathan that they'd probably be adopted into the tribe. "I hope they give us some meat when it's cooked," he remarked instead.

As soon as the fire burned down a little, the men sliced off pieces of meat and spitted them over the flames. Intent on their tasks, they took little notice of their captives. They had seemed to enjoy the earlier scuffling with Amos, teasing him as a cat teases a mouse, but now food was more important to them. Guessing the old man was their leader, Amos wondered if he'd ordered the prisoners left alone.

Amos stared at the venison, watching puffs of smoke rise from the dripping juices. The tantalizing aroma made his mouth water. The men tore off chunks of meat, crammed them in their mouths, then licked their greasy fingers. Their sounds of satisfaction were almost more than Amos could endure. But he was hesitant to ask them for some, for fear they would refuse him.

Amos saw Red Moccasin sitting by the fire, listening to the men talk. Again and again, his watchful gaze swung over to Amos, until finally he rose to his feet. Picking up two cooking sticks loaded with meat, he limped over and handed one of them to Amos, the other to Jonathan. Before Amos could even nod his thanks, the boy had turned back to the fire.

Though the venison was burned black, Amos tore into his portion, wolfing down bites, scarcely chewing them. He didn't even mind that the meat was almost raw in the middle. After days of near starving, it was a feast.

As Amos ate, he studied Red Moccasin. Bringing them the meat was a gesture of goodwill. Was the Indian trying to repay them for saving his life? Amos wished more than ever that they could talk to each other. Then he remembered that they were destined to become members of Red Moccasin's tribe. They'd have to learn the Indians' language in order to get by. He wondered if the day would ever come when he and Red Moccasin might be friends.

The Indians seemed in no hurry to travel on. They cooked and ate while morning turned into afternoon. Amos noticed the men putting some of the cooked venison in leather pouches and packs. As the day passed, the deer carcass was reduced to a shaggy hide and antlered head and a pile of discarded bones.

When one of the men brought them a second portion of meat in late afternoon, Amos warned Jonathan, "Don't eat it all now. Save some for later." He wrapped the remains of his piece in several green leaves.

"I'm still hungry," Jonathan said, stuffing another chunk into his mouth.

"You'll be hungry tomorrow, too," Amos told him.

Amos felt a tingle of fear when the old man and Red Moccasin came over and stood looking down at Clara. Amos tried to read the old man's face, but the cold, black eyes were as impenetrable as frosted windowpanes. An awful thought flashed into his mind. If Clara was unable to walk, the Indians might decide to take him and Jonathan and leave her behind.

When the old man and Red Moccasin walked away, Amos reached down and felt Clara's forehead. Her skin was still hot and dry. He held the cup of water to her lips, and for a moment, her eyes opened and seemed to focus on him. Then they closed again. Sick and weak from lack of food, she'd have no chance to survive alone. Amos made up his mind he wouldn't go on without her. If she couldn't walk, he'd carry her, no matter how far it was to the village.

By late afternoon, Amos had concluded that the Indians were waiting for someone. He was not surprised when four men walked up to the fire at dusk. They squatted there, talking to the others, accepting the cooked meat offered to them. When one of the men turned and looked full at Amos, a spark of recognition flashed between them. It was the man Amos had seen at Wheeling, the one who'd set the boat adrift, then at the last minute tried to snatch it back. Amos lowered his head to hide his thoughts. The man had attacked Wheeling, shot at his father, maybe killed him. Maybe all of the men here had been involved in that night assault.

As day passed into evening, the Indians let the fire burn low and stretched out among the rocks to sleep. They had no fear of their prisoners escaping, Amos knew, because there was one Indian guard out beyond the circle of firelight. Amos had seen him go.

Amos milked Queen Anne and after he and

Jonathan drank, they managed to coax Clara into taking a few sips. Then they raked together a pile of leaves for their bed. Jonathan soon drifted off, but Amos, his back against a rock, gazed into the fire.

He thought of the white boy the Shawnee had captured and named Blue Jacket. Had he stared into a fire that first night of his captivity and agonized over what would happen to him when he reached the Indian village? Learning to live with the Indians would be hard for them, Amos knew, but especially for Clara. She believed all Indians were savages, vicious and cruel. Amos wondered if living with them would change her mind.

Despite his worries, he began to relax and grow drowsy. There was a softness to the night, and a stillness, except for an owl screeching now and then in the distance. Amos was nodding and nearly asleep when he heard a noise. He looked up and saw the old man coming toward him. He waited, his heart thumping in his chest. The other Indians might tease him and steal his possessions, but this man would decide his fate.

Standing motionless between Amos and the fire, the man's features were a dark blur. His low-pitched voice startled Amos. "You lift boy from river."

Amos jerked upright when he realized he understood the words. "You speak English!" he blurted out.

The old man took a step nearer. "White man come to live in village. I teach him Shawnee. He teach me English."

So they were Shawnee, Amos thought, not that it mattered much. He and Clara and Jonathan were prisoners just the same.

"Why white boy lift Indian from river?"

Amos breathed out a long sigh. The man did not appear to be threatening him or trying to quarrel. He seemed almost curious. Red Moccasin must have told him about being saved from drowning. If he knows we saved the boy and doctored his wound, Amos thought, it might make a difference. He might let us go. With mounting hope, he spoke to the waiting Indian. "I couldn't let him drown."

"White man kills Indian." The statement was a simple, undeniable fact, Amos thought, but it sounded so . . . so hopeless. The old man must think all white men were killers, just as Clara thought all Indians were savages. Amos had no reply.

The old man sat down near Amos, crossed his legs, and folded his arms over his chest. In the fire's glow, his half-closed eyes were slits of reflected light. Just when Amos was beginning to think the man had gone to sleep, he pointed a crooked finger at Red Moccasin sleeping by the fire.

"He is son of my son. He is the last."

The old man's words seemed to hang there in the darkness until Amos untangled their meaning. The man was Red Moccasin's grandfather. That explained their familiarity, the easiness between them. Amos gazed at the boy sleeping on his side as Jonathan often slept, one hand cradling his cheek, the other tucked between his knees. Though he hadn't shown it, the boy must have been happy to see his grandfather. But Amos didn't understand about Red Moccasin being the last. Was he the last grandson, the last living child in the family, in the tribe?

Amos took a deep breath and asked the question. "What do you mean, Red Moccasin is the last?"

The old man swung around to peer at Amos in the dim light. He grunted, then asked a question in return. "Who is Red Moccasin?"

Expelling a noisy breath, Amos pointed at the Indian boy. "We can't say his name, so we call him Red Moccasin."

The old man sat silent a long time. He turned toward Amos once and seemed about to speak, but then looked back at the fire, his face stern and closed. His voice was almost a whisper when he did speak again.

"In season of ripe corn, white men kill the boy's father, mother, sisters. He run, he hide, but he sees it happen. He mourns many moons. Then he learns to hate."

The tale, told in a few blunt words, left Amos speechless. The boy had been forced to watch while white men killed his family. No wonder he looked on Amos and Clara and Jonathan as enemies. And in addition to losing everyone, he probably felt guilty because he'd been unable to help them.

The old man continued, his voice measured and low, vibrating in the darkness like the bass notes of a bullfrog. "He lost family. I lost family. Now we only ones left." His slitted eyes narrowed even more.

"We cross river to hunt in the land called Caintuck. White men attack. We run but we lose boy. We look for him many days." The man's gaze came back to Amos. "You lift boy from river. You not hate Indians."

It was a quiet declaration, yet Amos sensed the unspoken question. The man must have witnessed many deadly struggles between the white settlers and his own people, and Amos guessed he was trying to figure out why a white person would save an Indian's life.

"He was drowning," Amos said. "I couldn't let him drown."

"Indian is enemy of the white," the man insisted.

"I never saw him before in my life," Amos said. "How could he be my enemy?"

The old man seemed to ponder Amos's question, and after studying Amos for some time, he turned to gaze at the dying fire.

It came to Amos then that this might be his only opportunity to strike a bargain with the Indian before decisions were made that couldn't be undone. Blue Jacket's contract with the Shawnee had separated him forever from his family, and the same thing might happen to Amos. But he would accept it, if Clara and Jonathan were allowed to go free. Leaving them would surely be the hardest thing he'd ever have to do. He took a deep breath and stated his offer.

"I'll go with you and won't cause any trouble if you'll let my brother and sister go."

The man's reply came at once, firm and final. "You all go to village. All become Shawnee."

Anger sliced through Amos. The old man owed him something for saving Red Moccasin's life, and he was determined to collect that debt. Somehow, he knew that once they started for the village, there'd be no trade, no turning back. Maybe he could convince the old man that he really wanted to live with the Shawnee. It might not be so bad.

They would teach him how to live their way, and maybe in time he'd forget about his family.

"My brother and sister won't be happy at your village. But I will. I promise you, I'll learn to be a Shawnee, just like Blue Jacket."

"Blue Jacket! You know Blue Jacket?" The old man's eyes bored into Amos.

"No," Amos said, then hurried on. "But I want to go with you. Just let them go." He pointed to where Clara and Jonathan lay sleeping.

"Why you want to live with Shawnee?"

"Because . . . because I like Indian ways," Amos said. It was a lame answer, but maybe the old man would believe it.

"No. You tell true reason why you want to live with Shawnee."

Amos searched for an acceptable reply. "I want to live free, like the Shawnee," he said.

Still the old man waited, silent, unbelieving. Amos dropped his head and squeezed his eyes shut. There was more to this than just freedom for Clara and Jonathan, he had to admit. He was thinking of himself, hoping to run away from the hurting memory of Simon. But how could he confess all that to the old man? It would be better to make the Indian believe that he really wanted to be Shawnee.

Amos looked up, intending to lie once more, but the Indian's steady gaze stopped his words. The old man wasn't fooled. Fidgeting, unable to meet those knowing eyes, Amos realized that only the truth would do.

"Last year, I . . . I killed my best friend." He swallowed hard before continuing. "We were playing. I pretended to . . . to shoot him with a gun. I didn't know it was loaded."

The old man did not speak, but his gaze never left Amos's face.

Amos hurried on. "I thought if I went someplace where nobody knew me, I could forget about what I'd . . ." His voice cracked and trailed away.

A frown deepened the wrinkles on the old man's face, and his probing gaze touched Amos like a hot poker. Why had he told the Indian about Simon? He might have been able to live with the Indians without anybody knowing what he'd done. Now this man knew, and he'd surely tell the others. Well, it was done, but he had to make the old man understand. "I've tried to forget, but—"

The Indian's raised hand commanded silence. His stooped shoulders lifted and dropped as he took a deep breath, then he pointed at Red Moccasin. "My son's son carries spirits of family. He never lets them go. They are like a great stone on his shoulders. Each day the stone grows . . . gets bigger . . . gets heavier."

I know all about carrying such a burden, Amos thought. Every day he was reminded of Simon, sometimes of things they'd done together, sometimes of shared thoughts and feelings. But always, over all the remembrances, was the massive cloud of guilt. Red Moccasin had centered his hate on all white people, trying to erase his guilt. Amos had no one to blame but himself.

The old man's voice was soft beside him. "I tell boy, the spirits of dead walk a different trail. You hold them, they will not find trail. Must set spirits free."

There in the darkness, alone with the old Indian, the words sounded logical and wise. "But how?" Amos blurted out. "How can a person . . ."

The old man's eyes glittered in the firelight. "You say to spirit, our trails part. You say to spirit, I walk away."

Amos pulled his knees up until they touched his chin, considering the man's words. They puzzled him. They were so brief, so incomplete, yet they seemed to offer hope. He'd carried the sad memories of Simon for so many months, he didn't know if he could give them up. Besides, he wasn't sure how a person could lay aside such a burden and simply walk away.

He folded his arms across his chest and closed his eyes. He'd have to think on the old man's words when he was rested, when his mind was not so dulled with worry and fatigue and fear.

"You sleep now," came the Indian's quiet voice. He got up and returned to his seat by the fire.

Amos lay back beside Jonathan. An image of Simon appeared in his mind, not the pain-filled face of the last days, but the laughing face of earlier, happier times. He couldn't seem to live with the memory of Simon, yet how could he live without it?

Somewhere nearby, he heard a rustle in the leaves, the scurrying sound of some timid creature who slept in daylight and scavenged at night. Unlike that creature, Amos longed for the sun. Things always looked better in the bright light of day. As he drifted off to sleep, the old Indian's words whispered inside him like wind in tall grass. Walk away . . . walk away.

CHAPTER 13

Rumbling voices woke Amos, and scared him, too, when he remembered what had happened. He sat up and looked around. The fire had been rekindled and the men were squatting around it, talking as they held chunks of venison over the flames. Amos stood up and a passing Indian nodded to him, a greeting that seemed to say he was one of them now. Could he ever be Shawnee? Then, as he glanced down at Clara, Amos's breath caught in his throat.

Clara's eyes were open. They warmed with a weak smile. "What's happening, Amos? Where did they . . . ?"

Amos dismissed the Indians' presence with a wave of his hand. What mattered most was that Clara had beaten the fever. He grinned at her. "You've been out of your head for two days," he told her, reaching over to feel her forehead. "The fever's gone. The willow tea must have done it."

"Are they the ones we've been running from?" she asked, pointing to the men around the fire. She noticed the cow for the first time, and Jonathan sleeping beside her. "Thank goodness they're all right. Those savages had better not do anything to them or . . . ." She left her threat unspoken.

Amos felt a surge of relief. Clara's body might be weak, but her peppery spirit was still intact, and rising. "We'll be all right if we do what they say. They plan to take us to their village. The old man and Red Moccasin—"

"I knew we couldn't trust that Indian," Clara said, her eyes flashing in Red Moccasin's direction.

"The old man speaks some English," Amos said. "I talked to him last night." As he glanced at the Indians, he remembered the chunk of meat he'd saved. Removing the leaf wrapping, he saw that it had turned a gray, unappetizing color. Clara needed something better. "I'm going to get you some food," he said.

"Be careful, Amos. You can't . . . ."

Clara's voice faded away behind him as he approached Red Moccasin and his grandfather at the campfire. Amos stood before them, his gaze shifting from one to the other.

"My sister needs something to eat. Could I have a piece of meat for her?"

The other Indians by the fire ceased their activity, their eyes watchful but curious. One man pointed toward Clara, prompting the others to look.

Glancing back at his sister, Amos could see that she returned their stares with bold defiance. The look on her face gave Amos courage and he turned back to demand the food. But Red Moccasin was already there, handing him a stick of cooked venison. Nodding his thanks, Amos carried it back to Clara, grinning.

"You scared them into giving it to me," he teased.

"Oh, sassafras," was Clara's only comment before biting into the meat.

When Jonathan woke, they shared the meat and some of Queen Anne's milk, each swallow seeming to increase their strength and lift their spirits. But they were reminded of their predicament when the Indians began gathering up their few belongings. One man kicked the fire apart, sending white ashes billowing into the air.

"What are they doing?" Jonathan asked in a quivering voice.

"It looks as if they're getting ready to travel," Amos said. He glanced down at Clara. Even if she could walk, she wouldn't be able to walk far. When she gave out, he'd carry her, Amos resolved, because he was afraid of what the Indians might do if she couldn't keep up.

Just then, Amos saw Red Moccasin come toward him, speaking Shawnee words that sounded like a command. The boy must have been sent to get them moving. But Amos wasn't ready to go yet. He had to try once more to strike a bargain with the Shawnee.

"Just a minute," he said in a loud voice, catching everyone's attention, but fastening his eyes on the old man. "I ask you again to free my sister and brother. I'll go with you. Just leave them here." He waited, holding his breath.

"No!" Clara's single, scorching word spun Amos around. She was leaning against a tree trunk, her eyes blazing. "We all go free or we all go with them."

For a brief moment, Amos wondered how she'd found the strength to stand, let alone fight. "Stay out of this, Clara. I think I can get them to—"

"They can't separate us. I won't let them."

"Clara, be still. Maybe they'll let you and Jonathan go on to Marietta. Besides, I can learn their ways. I can be Shawnee." He bit his bottom lip. "Maybe living with them I can forget . . . about Simon." His last words were barely audible.

150

There was a breathless silence as Amos and Clara faced each other, everyone else there forgotten. Then Clara sagged against the tree, hugging her arms around her chest, her eyes smoldering. "Oh, Amos, there's no way to run from what you did. You'll carry it with you wherever you go."

Amos frowned, trying to recall what the old man had told him in last night's darkness. He hadn't said anything about running away from the blame. He'd talked about walking away. Amos wanted to try to reason out the man's words, but there wasn't time now. He had to convince the old man to leave Clara and Jonathan behind, despite Clara's objections. Ignoring her pleading eyes, he faced the Indian leader.

"I pulled Red Moccasin out of the river. You owe me something in return. Please . . . just let them go."

It seemed to Amos that Red Moccasin recognized the name they'd given him because he stepped forward to stand beside the old man. He might be able to persuade his grandfather to let them go, but would he? When Amos looked into the old man's flinty, unyielding eyes, he knew there'd be no help from anyone.

"All go live with Shawnee."

Hearing the finality in their leader's voice, some

of the men picked up their weapons and packs and went striding off through the trees. The Indian leader and Red Moccasin started after them.

"No! They stay here and I go with you," Amos called out, desperate to stop them and make them listen. But it was no use. They walked on as if he'd never spoken.

Amos turned back to Clara. "The old man might change his mind," he said.

Clara's eyes looked unusually large in her gaunt face. "No, he won't," she said, "but at least we'll be together."

An Indian motioned them on. Amos let Clara lean on him while Jonathan fell in behind them, leading Queen Anne. They had barely started when an odd sound from Jonathan made Amos turn around. One of the Indians had taken Queen Anne's lead rope and was untying it from the cow's neck.

"What are you doing?" Amos's voice was loud enough to stop everyone in sight. Ignoring Amos, the Indian worked the rope into a coil and slipped it over his shoulder.

"What are you doing?" Amos repeated even louder.

The Indian leader appeared at Amos's side. "Leave cow," he said in a matter-of-fact voice.

"What!" came Amos's shout, followed by an anguished cry from Clara. She ran and flung herself on Queen Anne, arms clasping the long, heavy neck. The cow, displaying her usual patience with humans, began to chew her cud.

"This animal is the only thing we have left." Amos's voice rose in protest. "We brought her all the way from Pennsylvania, and if you think you . . ." The hard expression on the old man's face made Amos pause. Realizing he was in no position to threaten anyone, his next words came out soft, pleading. "She can't get by on her own. She has to be milked every day . . . and watered."

Amos remembered hearing stories of families fleeing from hostile Indians, having to leave everything behind. When they returned to their homesteads, sometimes they would find their animals unharmed. Amos's father had explained why. The Indians were accustomed to a diet of wild game and had no use for the white man's livestock, for milk or meat.

Amos looked around at the waiting Shawnee. Most of them were burdened with heavy packs of deer meat. They seemed eager to be on their way, and he knew they would have no patience with a plodding cow.

"We go. Cow stay." The old man turned to resume

his place in line, but Clara's sudden explosion stopped him.

"I'm not going without her," she screamed. "I won't leave her. I won't!"

Amos took a step toward Clara, his breath tight in his chest. He wasn't sure what she might do, and he couldn't let her put them all in jeopardy. If their captors were determined to leave Queen Anne, neither he nor Clara could stop them.

"Amos, tell him . . . I won't leave her."

Again, Amos faced the Indian leader. "She raised the cow from a calf. The animal's more than just a—"

The old man wasn't listening. Instead, he turned to the man with the rope and gave a curt order. Without a moment's hesitation, the Indian stepped forward and laid the muzzle of his gun against Queen Anne's head.

For several seconds, Clara was too stunned to move. Then she screeched and lunged for the weapon. At the last moment, Amos grabbed her and dragged her away. As she slumped to the ground, he whirled toward the old man, hands outstretched, his voice hoarse. "Tell him not to shoot . . . don't hurt her. We'll leave her . . . just don't . . . ."

Suddenly, Red Moccasin appeared beside his

grandfather and began speaking to him in a low, urgent tone. The old man listened to him, asked a question in return, then nodded at the boy's response.

Amos held his breath, wondering whether the boy was interceding for them or urging his grandfather to kill the cow.

For a moment, the old man studied Amos. Then with a quick gesture to the man holding the gun, he turned and walked away.

Amos swallowed hard as he watched the Indian slowly lower the gun. He thought his legs were going to collapse under him. He clamped his jaws together and forced himself to stand erect. In that brief moment when his gaze met Red Moccasin's, Amos knew that the boy had saved Queen Anne.

Amos reached down and pulled Clara to her feet. They'd have to leave the cow but at least she'd be alive. "Come on. We've got to go without her. There's nothing else we can do."

Tears streamed down Clara's face. "Oh, Amos . . . how can we . . . what'll happen to her? I've always taken care of her."

Amos urged her ahead. "Here, put your arm around my waist and hang on to me." She tried to stop and turn back, but he wouldn't let her. He felt her feet dragging, as if she could barely lift them off the ground. "It's no use. You can't do anything," he said. "The old man won't change his mind."

The Indians strung out through the trees with Amos and Clara and Jonathan in the middle of the line. One Indian trod close behind them, at times almost bumping against Amos and Clara. Amos looked over his shoulder once and saw Queen Anne trailing at a distance. He hoped they would soon lose her, or she would give up following. If she continued after them, the old man might still order her shot.

They straggled up a steep hill and at the top, Clara pulled away from Amos to gaze back through the woods. Queen Anne was still visible among the trees, but she'd stopped to nibble at a low-hanging branch. Amos let out a silent breath of relief. She'd never catch up now.

Clara stood beside him, her hands clasped under her chin, her thin shoulders shaking. Near-starved and weak from the fever, Amos knew she had little strength left. The loss of Queen Anne might be more than she could endure.

"She's all alone," Clara said between ragged breaths. "She's never been alone in her whole life. She won't know . . ."

"Come on, Clara. There's no use looking anymore." Amos pulled her away, waving Jonathan ahead of him. "Maybe someone will find her." It was a feeble hope, he knew. There were thousands of miles of empty wilderness, and a lot more preying animals than people.

Clara seemed to walk in a daze, bumping into fallen logs, tripping over roots. Her glittering eyes made Amos fear that the fever had returned. No one uttered a word, not even the Indians, as the silent procession covered mile after mile, angling toward the sinking sun. The Ohio River lay far behind them now.

Afternoon had worn away to dusk by the time they stopped for the night beside a weedy stream. Soon after a fire was built, the pungent aroma of roasting venison scented the woods. The Indians didn't need to worry about the smoke, Amos mused, because this was their country.

He eyed Clara as she stretched out on her stomach, her face hidden in her arms. She wasn't concerned about the Indians, he knew, or what lay ahead for the three of them. She was thinking of Queen Anne.

Moving closer to the fire, Amos stared with longing at the cooking meat. He and Clara and Jonathan needed nourishment; if the men didn't give him some of the meat soon, he'd just take it. His fear of them was fading. After all, it wasn't likely they would harm persons they intended to adopt.

As if they'd read his thoughts, one of the men brought Amos a generous chunk of raw meat and indicated he should cook his own. That suited Amos. He'd make sure it was cooked just right.

After they'd eaten their fill, Amos wrapped the leftover meat in green leaves and placed it in Clara's knapsack. Then the three of them lay down to rest. They'd chosen a low place between two trees, not far from the fire. Though Amos couldn't see anyone outside the camp circle, he was sure someone had been assigned to guard them.

"What'll happen when we get to their village?" Jonathan asked.

"There's no need to worry," Amos murmured. "They're going to adopt us."

"Adopt us!" Jonathan exclaimed. "I don't want to be an Indian. I want to live with Papa."

"We don't have any say in the matter," Amos said. "Besides, we don't even know if . . . ." He stopped himself. Jonathan might as well go on believing their father was alive. He could be, for all they knew.

"I wonder how Queen Anne is," Clara said. "She must be awful lonesome."

"She may just find her way to Marietta," Amos said, hoping to cheer her. But the thought depressed him. If the cow did wander into Marietta and their father was there, he'd . . . . Don't think about that, Amos scolded himself. Think about surviving. The venison had strengthened him so that he felt almost like his old self again. Clara seemed to be improved, too. A good night's rest would prepare them for tomorrow's travel. He hoped Clara could sleep.

Amos opened his eyes, wondering what had wakened him. The fire had gone out, and it was so dark he couldn't see anything. He knew Clara and Jonathan were there beside him, though, because he could hear their breathing. Just then, somewhere off to his right, he heard a twig snap, then another. He held his breath and listened. Something was moving out there.

He leaned over to Clara and laid a hand over her mouth. She jumped at his touch, then lay still as he whispered in her ear. "I think there's somebody coming. Listen."

Motionless, breathing stopped, they waited. There was a stealthy sound, as if a branch had been brushed aside, then swung back into place. It could be the Indian guard on his night vigil, Amos thought, but he had a strange feeling of something closing in on them. He squeezed Clara's shoulder.

"Wake Jonathan, but don't let him make any noise."

Moments later, a light appeared, then another on the opposite side of camp. Suddenly, there were lights all around them, flaming branches flying through the air and falling amid the sleeping Indians.

The confused men awoke to the raining fire. They jumped to their feet, yelling, casting off fiery blankets. Gunshots cracked in the darkness.

Amos, Clara, and Jonathan flattened themselves on the ground as the sounds of fighting roared over the camp like a thunderstorm.

CHAPTER 14

≈≈≈≈≈≈≈≈≈≈≈≈≈≈≈≈≈≈≈≈≈≈≈≈≈≈≈≈≈≈

Caught between their captors and the unknown attackers, the three of them were helpless. The flaming branches must have burned out because Amos couldn't see anything now except the lightning flashes of the guns. The noise was deafening. He clapped his hands over his ears and burrowed into the leaves. When Jonathan started to lift his head, Amos pulled him back to the ground. "Stay down! We're in the crossfire."

Abruptly the gunshots ceased and a strange voice called out. "Don't let 'em get away." The sounds of English words ringing through the night made Amos catch his breath. He raised up on his hands and knees and shouted at the attackers. "Don't shoot. We're not Indians. We're—"

All of a sudden, it seemed that dozens of guns were turned on Amos alone. Bullets buzzed around him like angry bees, slicing through the leaves, chipping bark into his face. He threw himself to the ground. The attackers must have thought his call was an Indian trick. Just then, off to his left, he heard a man shouting, urging his men forward. "Get 'em all, boys! We don't want any of 'em coming back to Caintuck."

Amos guessed they were the same men who had attacked the old man's hunting party south of the Ohio. They must have trailed the Indians back into the Ohio country, bent on destroying them. There was no hope of rescue from such men.

The three of them lay there in their sheltered spot, their faces buried in the leaves, hearts pounding, throats dry with fear. As the furious conflict went on, Amos realized that the Indians were too busy fighting for their lives to worry about their prisoners. It might be possible for them to slip away unnoticed. He reached out and clasped Clara's arm.

"This is our chance to escape. They'll never see us in the dark."

"But they're all around us."

"Never mind," he whispered, knowing that with Clara so weak, he must be the leader now. "Just follow me. Go slow and keep your heads down," he told them. Then, stomach to the earth, he crawled out from between the two trees, his hands clawing at the moldy leaves.

Feeling his way through the murky woods, he hurried from one shadowy spot to another, like a mole shunning the light. Once they passed within a few feet of a flaming gun, but whether it belonged to a white man or an Indian didn't matter. Either one could mistake them for the enemy.

Amos's fear grew as he began to discern shapes around him, tree trunks and ferns and fallen logs. Dawn was not far off. They must find a hiding-place before the light came. He scurried on, pausing at last in a thicket of young saplings, some so close he could scarcely pass between them. Clara and Jonathan crept in beside him.

Amos ducked when he heard a bullet thud into a nearby tree. "Keep down. Dig under the leaves and hide," he whispered. "The sun'll be up soon."

Minutes passed that seemed like hours. At last Amos raised his head out of his leafy cave. He could distinguish the clear outline of a rock, then the pale gold of Clara's hair among the leaves. Smoke, a bluish haze against the green foliage, burned his nose and throat. He held his breath and listened. The gunshots were not as sharp and close as before. In fact, no sound came from their right, only from the left, and it was moving away. The battle seemed to have passed them by.

Amos brushed aside the damp leaves and scrambled to the edge of the thicket. They hadn't traveled far in the darkness because he spied the charred remnants of last night's campfire. There were no dead bodies, no injured in sight to remind them of the fierce fight that had taken place there. Clara and Jonathan came up beside him.

"Everyone's gone!" Clara's breathless words were both a question and a statement.

"Yes, but I can still hear them," Amos said, pointing in the direction of the muted sound.

"What do we do now?" Jonathan asked, his teeth clattering together. He clamped his jaws tight and lifted Clara's knapsack onto his shoulder.

"We get away from here as fast as we can," Amos said, already turning his back on the fading battle. He knew they must put distance between themselves and the warring parties.

He led the way at a fast pace until he realized that Clara hadn't the strength to keep up. Motioning Jonathan ahead, he went back to help her. She leaned on him, out of breath and unsteady on her feet.

"Do you think they'll come after us?" she asked him.

"The Indians are the only ones who know about us, and they're too busy right now. We've got to hurry and find the Ohio River."

"But how?" Clara asked. "We don't even know what direction we're traveling."

"I'm sure the river is still south of us," Amos said. "Once we get a fix on the sun, we can figure out where to go. But first we get away from here."

After walking for some time, they came to a shallow stream almost hidden by brush, but wide enough to let in the sun. The sky was a vibrant blue. Even before getting a drink, Amos picked up a stick about as big around as his thumb and pushed it into the ground. As the sun moved westward, the stick's shadow would fall eastward. Then when he pointed his right arm to the west and his left arm to the east, he'd be facing south.

By the time Clara was rested enough to continue, Amos had his bearings. They struck south, their spirits lifting with their new-found freedom and the knowledge that they were once more headed for Marietta.

Amos worried that they might veer off-course under the forest canopy, so at the top of a hill, he sent Jonathan up a tree to look for the river. Swaying among the flimsy top branches, Jonathan gave a yelp. "I see it. I see the Ohio. It's that way."

He pointed an arm to indicate the route they should take.

Amos helped Clara up. As they proceeded, she seemed to lean more heavily on him. After a while, he called a halt and told Jonathan to get the chunk of cooked venison out of the knapsack. It was cold and dry and a meager amount for three people, but it would give them some strength.

Amos looked down their back trail, wondering who had won the running battle between the Indians and the white men. For a moment, he thought of Red Moccasin. The Indian wasn't their concern anymore, but despite all that had happened, Amos still was glad that he'd pulled Red Moccasin out of the river. He hoped the boy had gotten away from the night attackers.

"How far are we from Marietta?" Jonathan asked.

"I don't know," Amos said, "but it can't be far. If the boatmen were right about the distances."

"Amos, we've got to find Queen Anne," Clara said. "I can't bear to think of her all alone in this wilderness."

"We need to get on to Marietta, Clara. Every minute we spend in these woods we're in danger. Besides, we could search for weeks and not find her."

"But she must be back there where we left her. She was at the bottom of a hill the last time we saw her."

Amos met Clara's worried gaze and shook his head. "We don't know where that is. We've got to go on to Marietta as fast as we can. Then someone there can come back and look for her. I'll come myself," he finished.

Clara hung her head. Her body shook and Amos knew she was crying. But he wouldn't give in. He couldn't! They were free and they had to get out of these woods before they were captured again.

Jonathan came and sat down beside Clara. "Don't cry, Sister. She'll get by until we find her."

Amos leaned down and laid his hand on the gold-crowned head. "Clara, it's only been a day. She's all right, and the sooner we get to Marietta, the sooner someone can come back for her."

Clara raised her head. She swiped at the tears running down her cheeks. "You're right, Amos. But I just hate to think . . . ." She stopped and her gaze flew past Amos and fastened on something behind him.

Watching her eyes widen, Amos felt a prickly chill crawl up his back. He sucked in a ragged breath and whirled around. There among the trees stood Red Moccasin.

Leaning to take the weight off his injured leg,

Red Moccasin gazed at them, his eyes glittering with a cold, determined light. Then he stepped forward and began to speak. When he paused and pointed off through the woods, Clara scrambled to her feet.

"Be careful, Amos. He's got a gun."

Amos barely took notice of her warning. The knowledge that Red Moccasin had survived the raid made everything else seem unimportant. After a few seconds, though, he began to wonder at the boy's presence. He wasn't surprised that Red Moccasin could follow their trail, because they hadn't tried to hide it. But why had he come after them?

Returning the Indian's gaze with as much calmness as he could muster, Amos asked, "What do you want?"

Red Moccasin spoke again, but this time shifted the gun into both hands. With deliberate care, he brought the barrel around until it pointed at Amos's chest.

Amos couldn't help but fall back a step. He didn't understand the Shawnee words but the boy's move was unmistakable. Red Moccasin was threatening them, and that threat could mean only one thing. He was bent on taking them back to his village, at the point of a gun, if necessary.

Staring at the gunbarrel's round, black mouth,

Amos felt a painful flutter in his stomach and he clamped his jaws so hard that his teeth ached. Had Simon felt this same kind of fear when he'd faced Amos's pistol? Not likely. Their confrontation had been pretend, a game between friends. But this was no game; Red Moccasin was deadly serious.

In the tense silence, fear swept Amos's mind clean, and resistance rose to take its place. After all they'd done for Red Moccasin, how could he threaten them with a gun! If they refused to go with him, what would he do? Shoot them?

"What do you want?" Amos asked again, stalling for time. Somehow there had to be a way to make Red Moccasin go away and leave them alone.

As the Indian boy again pointed through the woods, Amos took a step toward him, hands outstretched. "We can't go with you, Red Moccasin. We belong with our father. And you belong with your grandfather." Amos paused, then asked, "Where is your grandfather?"

A clear image of the old man edged into Amos's mind. Suddenly the Indian's counsel made sense to him. A person couldn't run away from his own history. But he could walk away, let go of the memory that haunted him. The old man had given him hope. Walk away. Maybe, Amos thought, I've already taken the first step.

"Where is your grandfather?" he repeated. "I'd like to thank him for . . . ." He stopped when Red Moccasin's expression changed. A shadow seemed to cross the Indian's face, like a cloud across the sun. Then his hand sliced through the air, as if to slap away Amos's question.

Amos's breath caught in his throat. He had his answer. The boy's grandfather had died in the fighting. "I'm sorry," Amos murmured. Though the boy couldn't understand the words, surely he could sense Amos's regret. With the old man gone, Red Moccasin was truly the last of his family.

Amos reached out a hand to this boy who was, despite the gun, still more friend than foe. But just as he took a step forward, the sound of a man's voice brought him to a halt.

"Hold on there, boy. Just stand real still until we sort this out."

As if in a dream, Amos turned his head and stared in the direction of the strange voice. A white man stood partially concealed behind a tree, his long-barreled rifle leveled at Red Moccasin.

While Clara and Jonathan stood staring at the man, too stunned to speak, Amos expelled a noisy breath. His first jubilant thought was that the man's presence meant freedom, safety, deliverance. But as he looked closer at the stranger, his joy began to melt. There was no sign of friendliness in the lean face. And the man's curt command ordering him to stand still had sounded almost like a threat.

Just as Amos took a cautious step toward Clara and Jonathan, he heard the click of a rifle hammer being cocked into firing position. He spun toward Red Moccasin. The Indian boy's weapon was just coming steady on the half-hidden stranger.

In the time it took to catch his breath, Amos figured out the dangerous conflict. Red Moccasin didn't want to give up his claim to the three of them. But the white man seemed determined to stop the Indian from doing anything. Maybe the man even meant to take Red Moccasin prisoner. Amos was sure that with a loaded gun in his hands, the boy would resist.

Somehow, Amos knew, it was up to him to end the standoff. Be careful! he warned himself. Guns kill, no matter who holds them. With shaking knees and hammering heart, he stepped forward until he stood between the two readied rifles.

CHAPTER 15

Amos held himself motionless as the man edged out from behind the tree. Deeply tanned, dressed in deerskin brown, the stranger could have been mistaken for an Indian.

"Move aside now," he told Amos. "That Indian may be a young one, but he's still a savage."

"You don't understand," Amos said, lifting a hand toward the man. "I know him. He's just a boy . . . like me."

The man's eyes narrowed on Amos. "He's Indian, and a minute ago he was ready to shoot you."

"He wasn't going to shoot me, Mister. He thinks it's his duty to take us back to his village."

"Well, the gun's aimed at me now, and either he puts it down, or I'm going to have to shoot him." The man's voice was cold and determined.

While Amos was trying to decide what to do, he saw a movement out of the corner of his eye. Clara laid a hand on Jonathan's shoulder for support and spoke to the stranger. "Please, Mister. Don't hurt Red Moccasin. He was drowning and my brother pulled him out of the river. We saved his life."

"That's right," Amos said. "We're . . . sort of friends."

"You can't be friends with an Indian." The man's mocking gaze slid past Amos to the boy. "Just step aside."

Anger welled up in Amos, swift and burning. He was sure he and Red Moccasin could be friends, if only they had the chance. They were more alike than the man could ever imagine. They'd both suffered great losses, and both believed the losses were their fault.

Amos glanced back at Red Moccasin. The boy's eyes showed no fear and no sign of giving in. Even as Amos watched, the Indian took a step sideways until his weapon was pointed once again at the stranger.

As much as Amos hated guns, he seemed unable to avoid them. But he hadn't pulled the Indian boy out of the river just to have him shot. Sucking in his breath, Amos stepped over until he stood in front of Red Moccasin again.

As he watched the stranger's hands tighten on his gun, Amos heard Clara muttering under her breath. She pushed past Jonathan and marched over beside Amos. With her hands on her hips and eyes flashing, she, too, faced the armed man. Only seconds passed before Jonathan joined them. In the stillness, they stood quiet, defiant, and united.

For several moments, the man stared at the three of them. Then he swung his rifle around until the barrel rested across his left arm. Gently he eased down the cocked hammer.

Amos released the breath he'd been holding and glanced back at Red Moccasin. The boy's weapon slowly dropped until the wooden stock touched the ground, though his eyes never left the stranger.

At last the man's voice broke the silence. "I know now why your father never gave up hope of finding you."

"You know our father!" Clara exclaimed. "You've seen him? Where is he? Is he . . . ?"

"Your name's Dunn, isn't it?"

"Yes, I'm Clara and these are my brothers, Amos and Jonathan. Where's our father? Why didn't he—"

"Your father's at Marietta," the man interrupted. "I have to tell you, he was wounded in the Wheeling raid. But he'll be all right," he hurried to add.

Amos and Clara and Jonathan beamed at each other. Their father was alive! Then they were all talking at once.

"We've been walking for days," Clara said.

"We were on the boat until . . ." Amos began.

"How'd you find us?" Jonathan piped up.

The man raised a hand and grinned. "I came across your trail along the Ohio, and wasn't far behind when the Indians captured you."

"They were taking us back to their village," Amos told him.

"I figured as much. I followed, hoping I might be able to get you away from them. But when your camp was attacked last night, I lost you. I trailed the Indians several miles before I realized you weren't with them."

"We got away in the dark and headed for the Ohio," Amos said.

"I know. I came back to the campsite and found your trail. I would've caught up with you sooner but I ran into the cow and she slowed me down."

"You found her! You found Queen Anne!" Clara's eyes flooded, wide and bright.

"Sure did," the man said. He waved a hand over his shoulder. "She's back there in the trees."

Looking in the direction he pointed, they saw Queen Anne just emerging into the open, head up, ears wide. Clara rushed over and hid her face against the cow's neck, her tear-filled voice murmuring words only Queen Anne could hear. Jonathan went too, and stroked the Jersey's soft, moist nose.

Amos looked at the man, trying to explain. "We've had her since she was a calf. The Indians made us leave her behind."

"She's a friendly thing," the man said, grinning. "Took to me straight away and followed right along."

As she urged Queen Anne forward, Clara's eyes glowed like polished copper. The news of their father and the reunion with the cow, one so close on the other, had left her speechless. But Amos asked the question they all wanted answered. "How far is it to Marietta?"

"If you young 'uns are up to a good walk, we'll eat supper there tonight."

Tears filled Amos's eyes and he dropped his head so the man wouldn't see.

"By the way," the man said, "my name's Rufus Caine."

"Are you an Indian fighter?" Jonathan asked him.

"Everyone in the Ohio country is an Indian fighter at one time or another," Rufus said. "When the Indians are quiet, I work as a surveyor for the government."

"You must be good at tracking," Jonathan said.

"I've had a little practice," Rufus replied with a grin. He turned to gaze at Red Moccasin leaning against a tree. "That young Shawnee's probably twice as good at tracking as I am. They start learning as soon as they can walk."

Red Moccasin must have known they were talking about him, but no trace of his thoughts showed on his face.

"What on earth prompted you to pull him out of the river?" Rufus asked Amos.

"That question's been asked before," Amos said, his gaze flicking toward Clara. "I guess I just couldn't stand by and watch a person drown."

"You'll have to be careful who you befriend here in the Ohio country. There's no Indian can be trusted."

Amos didn't want to argue with Rufus Caine, but he didn't doubt for a minute that he could trust Red Moccasin. He wished he could speak Shawnee, tell the boy he was sorry about his grandfather. I'd like to tell him how his grandfather helped me, Amos thought. He turned back to Rufus. "Do you speak Shawnee?"

"Never had a chance to learn," the man said. "Every time I meet up with a Shawnee, he's pointing a gun at me."

Amos's gaze swung back to Red Moccasin. The dark eyes met Amos's, as unreadable as ever, but the stony expression didn't intimidate Amos. He knew why the boy distrusted white people. If they had more time, he was sure he could make Red Moccasin understand that they were alike in many ways. Maybe one day he could even tell the boy about Simon. But time had run out.

"I reckon the best thing to do is let your Shawnee friend go back to his village," Rufus said to Amos. "Can you make him understand?"

Amos nodded. "He doesn't know the words, but he gets the meaning."

Amos walked over and stood before Red Moccasin, lifting a hand to point off through the woods. "You can go home now." When the boy didn't move, Amos stretched out his arm, pointing with all his fingers as he'd seen Red Moccasin and the other Indians do. "You go," he said. The boy continued to stare at Amos, even when Clara and Jonathan appeared beside them.

"He doesn't understand you," Clara said.

"I think he does, but he's got something else on his mind."

There was a spark in Red Moccasin's eyes as he looked at the three of them, a gleam that Amos thought might be a trace of understanding, even acceptance. The Indian spoke at last, almost in a whisper, and though the words were alien, Amos sensed the boy's true intention.

"What's he saying?" Clara asked.

"I believe he's thanking us for saving his life."

"Well, it's about time," she said.

Amos smiled at her remark, his eyes still on Red Moccasin. A twitch of the Indian boy's lips told Amos that he'd understood Clara's wry comment, but chose to ignore it.

Just then, the boy bent down and pulled something from the top of his moccasin. Amos's eyes widened. It was his marble pouch! The marbles were still inside—he could hear them rattling together. Red Moccasin handed the pouch to him.

"How'd he get that?" Clara asked.

"Someone took it from me when we were first captured," Amos said. "I never thought I'd see it again." He grinned at Red Moccasin. "I thank you. I don't know how you ended up with it, but I thank you for giving it back."

Rufus stepped over beside Amos. "The Shawnee rarely give back something they've taken from you. This boy honors you, Amos."

"I wish I could tell him . . . well, I'd like to tell him a lot of things." As Amos tied the pouch to his belt, he thought of Simon and the games of marbles they'd played. There'd be no more games with his lost friend, but he could make new friends. He loosened the drawstring and reached in, curling his fingers around Simon's green agate shooter. Its touch no longer burned. When he pulled it out, it lay in his open palm, cool and smooth and bright.

Amos looked up at Red Moccasin and smiled, then reached out the hand holding his shiny gift.

There was surprise in Red Moccasin's face, but it soon gave way to a hint of a smile. He took the green marble from Amos's hand, locking his fingers tightly around it. For a moment, the closed hand rested against his chest, then he raised it upright at his shoulder. It was a gesture of thanks, Amos guessed, but it was also farewell, and something more . . . respect, maybe. Then, cradling his rifle in one arm, Red Moccasin turned and walked off.

As Amos watched him fading away through the woods, he knew the boy would not look back. He'd said his goodbye, and now his thoughts were turned toward home. He still walked with a limp, but Amos was confident he would make it back to his village. After all, he knew these woods.

Amos wrapped a hand around the marble pouch. In returning the marbles, Red Moccasin had opened the closed door between them. Maybe in giving him Simon's shooter, Amos had planted a seed of friendship. He hoped it would take root. He sent a single, fervent thought winging after the Shawnee. If ever we should meet again, Red Moccasin, I intend to greet you as a friend.

"I reckon we should get going," Rufus said. "The sun's got a head start on us."

"Let's hurry," Clara said, nudging Jonathan ahead of her.

"I thought you were sick," Jonathan said.

"All of a sudden I'm better," his sister replied, her eyes sparkling with the familiar, sassy gleam.

They set off in single file, Jonathan behind Rufus Caine, then Clara leaning on Queen Anne, and Amos last.

Once more they were headed for Marietta, Amos thought, but now they had a guide. They were safe and free and they'd see their father before the sun set. The cool, dim woods were as silent as ever, but their dangers seemed to fade with every step Amos took. The Ohio country was beginning to feel like home.

AUTHOR'S NOTE

America's early colonies claimed lands extending far to the West, but after the Revolutionary War, they yielded most of this land to the new government. Virginia stretched from the Atlantic Ocean all the way to the Ohio River. It maintained that western boundary until West Virginia was made a state in 1863.

Even before the United States acquired the western territories, people were exploring and settling north of the Ohio River. Indians living there—the Shawnee, Mingo, Wyandot, Miami, and Delaware tribes—resisted, but finally were forced to give up most of southern and eastern Ohio. Settlers poured into the wilderness, using the Ohio River as a highway to the West. Ohio became a state in 1803.

The early settlers were hardy and independent, and lived off the land. Children were a vital part of the frontier family. They helped harvest wild foods, nuts, berries, tender and nutritious nettle tops, sassafras for tea. The frontier family relied on wild herbs and medicinal plants such as comfrey, pennyroyal, willow, and chickweed to treat illnesses and injuries.

Wild animals, fish, and fowl were a major part of the frontier diet. Carolina parakeets, birds which did not migrate, lived in large flocks year round in the river bottoms as described in the story. Not only were these birds good to eat, but their brightly colored feathers were valued for decorations, and they were often trapped and sold as cage birds. Because of excessive hunting and loss of wilderness nesting sites, the Carolina parakeet, the only parrot native to North America, was extinct by the late 1800s.